"What exactly are you most afraid of?" he mocked

Craig stared into Rachel's eyes as if searching for an answer there. "Or should I say who?"

"Whom?" she corrected with deliberation. "And it isn't fear I'm feeling so much as revulsion. If Charles had known you better, he'd never have asked it of me!"

"Fear I said and fear I meant," came the calm insistence. "The response I roused in you earlier shook you to the core, didn't it? You'd never known it could be like that—especially with a man you don't even like, much less love.

"Deny it all you like, but there's a real live woman in there somewhere. Charles might have treated you like Dresden china, but I've no such intention."

KAY THORPE, an English author, has always been able to spin a good yarn. In fact, her teachers said she was the best storyteller in the school—particularly with excuses for being late! Kay then explored a few unsatisfactory career paths before giving rein to her imagination and hitting the jackpot with her first romance novel. After a roundabout route, she'd found her niche at last. The author is married with one son.

Books by Kay Thorpe

Don't miss any of our special offers. Write to us at the following address for information on our newest releases.

Harlequin Reader Service
P.O. Box 1397, Buffalo, NY 14240
Canadian address: P.O. Box 603,
Fort Erie, Ont. L2A 5X3

KAY THORPE

THORPE

Left in Trust

Harlequin Books

TORONTO • NEW YORK • LONDON
AMSTERDAM • PARIS • SYDNEY • HAMBURG
STOCKHOLM • ATHENS • TOKYO • MILAN
MADRID • WARSAW • BUDAPEST • AUCKLAND

Harlequin Presents first edition July 1993
ISBN 0-373-11571-7

Original hardcover edition published in 1992
by Mills & Boon Limited

LEFT IN TRUST

CHAPTER ONE

'ARRIVING Cowes 3.00 p.m. ferry the 4th' was all the mailgram had said.

That surely meant as a foot passenger expecting to be met, Rachel reflected, watching the stream of people dwindle down to the odd one or two, with still no sign of the man. The family album had supplied a recent enough photograph to ensure recognition, so she was sure she hadn't missed him. Either he had missed the ferry altogether, or he had come over with a car, in which case he could have driven past without her spotting him.

In the latter case, he was the one at fault for not making things clearer, she told herself. Brevity was no doubt a stock-in-trade where journalism was concerned, but surely not at the cost of clarity?

With the last of the arriving passengers disembarked, and the Southampton bound beginning to board, there was no point in waiting around any longer. Rachel made her way back to where she had left the car, shrugging wry shoulders at the grey-uniformed man who got out to open the rear door for her.

'Seems there's been a mix-up,' she said. 'He wasn't on the ferry.'

'I dare say Mr Lindhurst will find his own way to Apperknowle in due course, milady,' replied the chauffeur expressionlessly.

Rachel slid into her seat, automatically pulling in the folds of her pleated red skirt as Grayson closed the door on her. The smooth, soft leather gave off a familiar and

5

expensive aroma, complementing the expanse of polished walnut. Up until a couple of years ago, she had rarely even seen a Rolls-Royce, much less driven in one.

Considering the island's narrow and crowded roads—the latter in season, at least—it wasn't the ideal vehicle in which to ride around at all, but she couldn't bring herself to get rid of it as yet. The car was a symbol of Charles's success; it held an essence of the man she had loved so dearly. She had learned to live with her loss over the past months, and to adjust to the idea of supplanting him with another. Whether Craig Lindhurst would see things quite the same way remained open to question. A dying man's last wishes might well mean little to one as inured to human suffering as a hard-bitten foreign-affairs journalist must be.

'Back to Apperknowle, milady?' enquired Grayson, taking the wheel.

'Yes, home, please. He might even have come in on an earlier ferry, and be there already.'

Leaning back in her seat as the chauffeur put the car into motion, Rachel tried to sort out exactly what she was going to say to the newcomer when they did eventually come into contact. All Craig Lindhurst knew so far was that he stood to inherit one half of his uncle's entire estate. It was the condition governing that inheritance that was likely to throw a spanner in the works. How many men faced with such a choice would simply accept it?

The vast majority, the cynical part of her mind supplied. The loss of a certain amount of freedom was surely a small price to pay for such a return? She herself stood to pay the highest price, but a promise made in such circumstances was inviolable. The Lindhurst name and Apperknowle had been linked for the last two hundred years. It had been Charles's dearest wish that the link should continue. Given a little more time, none of this might have been necessary. Only time had run out on them that October morning six months ago.

Rachel blinked hard on the involuntary moisture gathering at the back of her eyes. Charles would have hated her to weep for him. They'd had almost a whole year of happiness together—more than anyone could have anticipated considering. Life had to go on. Apperknowle had to go on. If Craig Lindhurst failed to meet the requirements of their joint inheritance, all would be lost. She *had* to convince him!

Drawing up the mirror from the top of the built-in cabinet in front of her, she checked for tell-tale signs of smeared mascara. The reflection showed a face more striking than merely pretty, with its high cheekbones and wide-spaced vivid blue eyes. Her long, honey-blonde hair was at present swept up into a smooth french pleat, making her look older than her twenty-three years. There were times, she thought now on a note of wry humour, when she felt a great *deal* older than twenty-three. This was one of them.

Once past the double iron gates of Osborne House, they were soon out into open countryside, fresh and green under the afternoon sun, with the gentle slope of the downs forming a not too distant horizon. Born and bred here on the island, Rachel had never at any time felt restricted by the lack of wide open spaces. The mainland was close enough for visiting on a regular basis if one felt the need, and close enough for commuting on a daily basis where work called the tune.

Landing the job with Charles so soon after finishing her training had seemed like manna from heaven at the time, though she knew now, of course, that her secretarial abilities had taken second place to her potential in other spheres. Some might consider that Charles Lindhurst had set about finding a mother for the child he had hoped to father with little caution. Some might even find the whole idea objectionable.

She herself had been devastated initially by the total honesty of his approach to the subject. Had circumstances been different, he had admitted, he would never have presumed on the closeness which had developed between the two of them, no matter how much he might have wanted it. Things being the way they were, however, he'd been left with no choice but to seize what opportunity might be offered him.

Had she not felt the way she did about him by then, she wouldn't have been able to go through with the marriage, Rachel knew. Loving a man almost forty years older than oneself might seem strange to some, but loved him she had. Steel-haired, distinguished and looking far less than his age, regardless of his illness, he had been one of the kindest, most trustworthy men she had ever known. A replacement in some ways for the father she had lost in her early teens, perhaps, but also a husband to cherish.

The marriage had caused a stir of the kind with which her mother had found difficulty in coping. Rachel's failure to conceive the child for which Charles had craved had been greeted with a measure of relief by her surviving parent. Laura Howard was not aware of the condition Charles had laid down for inheritance to go through. Nor, Rachel hoped, was it going to be necessary for her to know.

Charles had stipulated a time lag of no more than a year between his death and her marriage to his nephew. If tracing Craig's whereabouts hadn't taken so long, they could have taken advantage of the full term to get to know one another before sealing the contract. With barely six months to go, the affair was going to cause adverse comment whichever way it was handled.

Something which would have to be dealt with as and when, she thought with firmness. Other people's opinions were of relatively minor importance.

They were coming into Newport via streets nowhere near as busy now in early April as they would be in a month's time, but enough so to call for extra care and attention on Grayson's part.

'There appears to have been an accident,' commented the latter as they approached the first junction. 'Two vehicles involved, by the look of it.'

Rachel leaned forward to look through the windscreen at the scene ahead. One car—a Jaguar—was slewed sideways by the impact of the other saloon, its front offside wing crushed inwards on to the wheel. Racing the lights, she judged. As both drivers were out in the road being interviewed by a policeman, there at least appeared to be no serious human injury.

One of the male drivers was giving a loud and vehement account of the accident, while the other stood listening without comment. Tall, dark, and wholly in command of himself, he drew instant recognition on Rachel's part.

'You'd better pull in and wait,' she instructed Grayson, reaching for the nearside door-handle. 'That would appear to be our man!'

A small crowd had gathered on the pavement. Rachel pressed through to reach the threesome still engaged in sorting out the whys and wherefores. The policeman was young and well-built, with black curly hair and an irrepressible twinkle lurking in his eyes. She smiled at him.

'Hello, Keith. Sorry to interrupt, but I was supposed to meet Mr Lindhurst here at the ferry fifteen minutes ago. He's Charles's nephew.'

Keith Barratt touched the peak of his cap with a deference that was just a touch mocking, though lacking in malice. 'Good of you to stop, milady. It seems we have a case of joint liability.'

'It wasn't my fault, I tell you!' expostulated the man who had been doing all the talking so far. He——' jerking his head in Craig Lindhurst's direction '—came through on the amber!'

'We both did,' returned the other levelly. 'A bad habit we should both watch in future. Luckily we got away with it this time.' He lifted an enquiring eyebrow at the representative of the law. 'Always considering what action you might feel bound to take, of course, Officer?'

Keith studied him for a brief moment, then shrugged and closed his notebook. 'I'll have to put in a report, but I don't imagine there'll be any action taken as there were no injuries. As you said, just keep a sharper eye open from now on.' He cast an expert eye over the two vehicles still half blocking the road. 'You'll need a tow-wagon to shift the Jag very far, I'd say, but we can at least get it in to the side out of the way for the time being.' He shook his head as Rachel moved forward to lend a hand in pushing the vehicle, the grin only half concealed. 'No job for a lady.'

'Stow it,' she said sweetly, and saw the grin break full cover.

'Anything you say, ma'am!'

'He's right,' stated Craig Lindhurst on an unequivocal note. 'It's no job for a lady—of either kind.'

Blue eyes clashed with steely grey: sudden flaring animosity crackled between them. For a brief moment

Rachel was on the verge of telling this man exactly where to get off, before memory supplied a reason for keeping the cart on the wheels. She needed his goodwill, not his enmity.

Summoning a smile, she made a gesture of assent. 'I'll wait in the car. You're going to need transport after you sort things out. Any objections, Keith?'

'Not providing you move it further down off the yellow lines,' he said.

Craig was already bending his back to the task of separating the two vehicles, with the help of a couple of men who had stepped from the crowd. Rachel gave the young constable another warm smile. 'How's Lindsay and the baby?'

'Fine,' he said. 'Why don't you come over some time, and see for yourself?'

'I'd love to.' She meant it. There was a whole lot more she would have liked to say, but this was neither the time or place. Her old friends had been sadly neglected this past eighteen months. Mostly because they themselves had shown little desire to stay in contact after she had married Charles. 'Tell her I'll phone,' she added.

Grayson moved the car back to the appropriate place as soon as she was inside, and she settled down for a lengthy wait. Rachel could feel the aggression still simmering deep down. Craig Lindhurst might have something of his uncle's looks and bearing, but he was nothing like him in temperament—that much she couldn't be more sure of.

And this was the man she was supposed not only to marry, but to have a child by! Right up until this moment she hadn't allowed herself to contemplate the obvious and necessary factors involved in that procurement. Charles was the only man she had ever known that way—

the only man she could imagine knowing that way. The very thought of any physical relationship with his nephew was suddenly anathema to her. How could she even begin to consider it?

The other man's car proved driveable. After exchanging insurance details, he left the scene. It was another half an hour before the pick-up truck arrived. Craig waited for it in the Jaguar.

From where she sat, Rachel could see the back of the dark head through the rear screen. He could have spent the time in the Rolls, but that was obviously not his wish. The animosity had not been one-sided; he no more wanted to talk to her than she did to him.

Only they were going to have to talk eventually—and sooner rather than later. There was nothing to be gained from trying to hide the relevant detail. Rachel wasn't sure it would be legal even to attempt to do so. The best way might be simply to show him a copy of the will and let him realise the implications for himself. Less embarrassing, certainly, than trying to put it into words of her own.

With the Jaguar finally on its way, Craig carried his suitcase back to the Rolls, handing it over to Grayson to stow away in the boot before sliding into the rear seat alongside Rachel. Even sitting, he seemed to tower over her, his very presence in the car so overpoweringly masculine. The lean features looked chiselled from stone.

'Hardly an ideal way to meet,' he commented without particular regret. 'I've been to Apperknowle before, by the way.'

'I'm aware of it, but you didn't make it clear whether or not you'd have transport,' she replied levelly. 'I was waiting at the dock. You must have driven past me.'

He gave her a frankly appraising scrutiny, dwelling for a brief moment on the soft fullness of her mouth before coming back to meet her eyes with a sardonic little smile touching his own well-cut lips. 'I wouldn't have recognised you for who you are. You're even younger than I anticipated.'

'You must have known my age before this,' she returned, and despised herself for the defensive note she had allowed to creep in.

The slant of his lip became rather more pronounced. 'I wasn't referring to years.'

Rachel rallied herself, eyes taking on a coolly calculating light. 'At thirty-four, you're not exactly in your dotage yourself.'

'Unlike my uncle.'

'Sixty isn't ancient either!'

'It is when it comes to marrying a girl scarcely out of the cradle.' His tone was unrelenting. 'Not that you were behind the door when it came to realising the advantages. You knew he was dying when you agreed to marry him, of course.'

Grayson was coming back to get behind the wheel. Rachel leaned forward and slid the sound-proofed screen across before deigning to answer the implied accusation. 'If you're suggesting I only married him because I knew there was a time-limit on the arrangement, you're quite wrong. Charles was a man in a million!'

'He was also very rich,' came the smooth reply.

She drew in a ragged breath. Craig Lindhurst wasn't the first to think that way, and he wouldn't be the last, but it still hurt to be classed as nothing but a fortune-hunter. 'Your outlook is obviously coloured by your job,' she said scathingly. 'An out-and-out cynic! I might have expected nothing else from you.'

The car was in motion now, the movement smooth and almost soundless. Craig studied her again, taking his time about it, eyes unrevealing. 'You're telling me you were in love with a man old enough to be your grandfather?'

Rachel had never thought of it that way. The fact had no bearing even now. Charles had been Charles. Just that. Neither his age nor his title had affected her emotions. Not that she expected this man at her side now to believe it. He would believe whatever he wanted to believe.

'I'd suggest we leave that subject alone,' she said with control. 'It isn't something I care to discuss with you. You're here to claim your share in the estate.'

'I'm here,' he retorted, 'to learn why an uncle I've seen nothing of over the years since my father died should have singled me out to benefit from his will at all.'

'I'd have thought that was obvious,' Rachel rejoined. 'You bear the name Lindhurst.'

'So does my brother.'

Blue eyes darkened. She said slowly, 'I didn't know there was a brother. Charles never mentioned it.'

He gave her a reflective look. 'But he did mention me?'

'Well, yes.' She shook herself mentally. 'Older or younger—the brother, I mean?'

'What else?' The sarcasm was muted. 'Gary's twenty-six.'

'A journalist too?'

'No, he works for a stockbroker firm.'

'A yuppie?' Rachel regretted the snide comment the moment she had made it, seeing the derision with which it was received.

'You're out of date. The upwardly mobile are presently cruising in the slow lane. Gary's no exception.'

'Well, at least you'll be in a position to help him out,' she said in an attempt to retrieve the situation.

'So it appears.' He sounded sceptical. 'I can't believe it's that straightforward. As Charles's widow, you were entitled to inherit the lot. I'm surprised you haven't taken steps to contest the will.'

Rachel could feel her face freeze. Her voice when she spoke was taut. 'Whatever Charles wanted is fine with me. I wouldn't dream of contesting his wishes in any sphere!'

'Very commendable.' There was no doubting the irony in his voice. 'Sharing with a stranger isn't going to be easy.'

Especially considering the extent of that sharing, she thought in growing disquiet. Everything about this man set her teeth on edge. How on earth could she reconcile herself to the physical intimacy which would be part and parcel of the partnership, should he agree to the condition? For the first time she found herself half hoping that he would turn the whole thing down—although, by virtue of her promise to Charles, she had to try her best to persuade him to go along with it.

They were through Calbourne and heading for Brighstone Forest. Another ten minutes would see them at Apperknowle. Home for the next six months, whatever happened. The memory of what was to come after that, should the terms of **the will** not be met, brought heaviness to her heart. Two hundred years of history down the drain. It didn't bear thinking about.

Craig was gazing out of his side-window at the passing landscape, face set in lines impossible to read. She would have given a great deal to know exactly what he was thinking and feeling at the moment. Not that she anticipated any more generous assessment where she herself was concerned. He had made his opinion on that score only too devastatingly clear.

Shimmering beneath the bright blue sky, the sea came into view. One or two sails were visible in the middle distance, while further out could be seen the shape of some larger vessel turning stern on to the island as it headed down the Channel. Rachel had this same view from her bedroom windows, and she loved it. Were she forced to leave the manor eventually, it was only one of the things she would miss. Apperknowle had become as dear to her as it had been to Charles, and he had known it, which was why he had placed such trust in her.

She would fight tooth and nail, she told herself fiercely, to merit that trust.

The wrought-iron gates guarding Apperknowle from the outside world opened smoothly to the touch of a button on the control in Grayson's charge. Tree-lined and winding, the drive ran for several hundred yards before the house came into sight. Built around 1750 by a Lindhurst renowned as much for his successful gambling as his business acumen, it had a classic Georgian frontage, with rows of tall windows and a pillared entrance porch. The stonework had mellowed over the years to a warm gold, welcoming now in the sunlight.

Mostly running to parkland at the front, the main gardens lay to the rear of the house, along with the heated swimming-pool Charles himself had installed, and a croquet-lawn Rachel had learned to appreciate. Seeing the place up close for the first time the day of her interview, she had fallen in love with it immediately. Big and imposing as it was, it had felt like a home.

'It might have been yesterday,' remarked Craig softly as they rounded the final bend. 'Nothing changes.'

'How long *is* it since you were last here?' Rachel asked for want of anything more riveting to say.

'Ten years, give or take a few months. My father and Charles went their separate ways early on.'

'After Charles inherited?'

He gave her a swift, hard glance. 'As eldest son, he had the right by tradition. Dad was left neither destitute nor rancorous, if that's what you're thinking.'

'I'm glad to hear it.' Rachel had no intention of apologising for the implication. If Craig could judge on the basis of supposition, there was no reason why she shouldn't do the same. 'Now the wheel turns back again. What he lost, you gain.'

'Not wholly,' came the cool reminder. 'At present the Lindhurst name still holds the monopoly, true, but I wonder if Charles gave any serious thought to what will happen if and when you marry again?'

Rachel felt her heart give a painful thud. 'Yes, he did,' she got out with creditable control, and saw the dark brows rise.

'How exactly? A change of name by deed poll? That might limit your choice of partner. Not all men would be willing.'

They were drawing up beneath the porticoed entrance. Rachel seized on the excuse not to answer that question in full. 'All will be revealed,' she said, gathering herself for a swift exit before Grayson could come and perform that function of his job which she found so unnecessary while she was capable of opening her own doors. 'We'll talk over tea.'

Craig followed her out of the car, leaving the chauffeur to get back behind the wheel with a philosophical shrug and head for the coach-yard off to one side of the house. The entrance hall was large, imposing and also boasted Georgian pillars framing an alcove in which was set a marble bust of the Roman Emperor Tiberius. The floor was carpeted now in thick, plum-coloured Wilton, covering the original freestone flags inset with black marble. Too cold, Charles had declared.

Rachel smiled a greeting to the middle-aged and pleasant-featured woman in blue who appeared from the rear premises. 'You'd be here ten years ago, wouldn't you, Mrs Brantley? You remember Mr Lindhurst?'

'Of course.' The woman gave the newcomer a respectful nod. 'Welcome back, sir.'

'Thank you.' The scorn was faint enough to go unnoted by anyone not watching the line of his mouth—which Rachel was.

'We'll have tea in the library, please,' she said. 'Unless you'd rather freshen up first?' she added to Craig. 'Grayson will have taken your case up the back way.'

'It might be an idea,' he agreed. 'I only stopped off from the airport to pick up some clothes and the car before heading down here. Aircraft toilets leave a lot to be desired.'

'Tea in half an hour, then,' Rachel instructed the housekeeper. 'I'll show Mr Lindhurst his room myself.'

A minor reprieve, but still a reprieve, she thought as they mounted the oak staircase together. She dreaded the coming disclosure. Trying to imagine Craig's reaction to Charles's decree was a futile exercise. She would learn in good time how he felt.

The bedroom she herself had chosen for Craig was at the rear of the house, like her own. Decorated in blue and white, with rich mahogany furnishings, it boasted a four-poster bed and had its own adjoining bathroom.

The leather suitcase already resided on a stand at the foot of the bed.

'Nice,' commented Craig. 'A bit different from what I've been used to these past few months.' He made no attempt to enlarge on that statement. 'How many staff do you employ?'

'How many staff do *we* employ,' Rachel corrected levelly. 'Six, if you count the two gardeners.'

'All living in?'

'Hardly. Mrs Brantley has her own room, of course, and Grayson has a flatlet over the stables; the rest come in on a daily basis.'

'All local?'

'They could scarcely be anything else on an island twelve by twenty-one.'

'Point taken.' If he registered the sarcasm, he wasn't rising to it. 'I'm not used to thinking in terms of restricted access.' He moved across to the nearest of the two tall, silk-draped windows to gaze out over the impressive view. 'At least this isn't. Restricted, I mean. There's many who'd pay the earth to have all this on their doorstep.'

With his back turned to her, there was nothing to stop Rachel running her eyes over the lean length of him. The shoulders beneath the tan suede bomber-jacket were broad, his hips narrow by comparison, the whole concept one of firm muscularity and latent power. A man who kept himself in strict fighting trim, she judged, and was aware of a certain gathering of tension in the region of her stomach. Dislike him as a person though she might, the masculine charisma was undeniable. She wouldn't be the first woman to feel it by a long way.

'Except that it isn't for sale,' she said a little too quickly. Not yet, came the mental rider. She added abruptly, 'I'll leave you to it. The library is first on the right as you come downstairs.'

He turned then to give her a suddenly narrowed glance. 'I dare say I'll find it OK.'

As he was a man who spent much of his life in strange and often hostile places, Rachel could imagine that Apperknowle would present little problem. *Her* problem over the next twenty minutes or so was finding the kind of insouciance that would carry her through what promised to be a harrowing revelation. Craig had already made it obvious that he suspected all was not quite as straightforward as it might appear.

The library was her favourite room in the house. Lined in oak, and with two whole walls bearing loaded bookshelves, it was large enough to do double duty as a second sitting-room, yet cosy too. Because the April sunshine still lacked any real heat, a fire had been lit in the wide stone hearth, fed with apple logs, which gave off a delightful scent.

Seating herself in one of the chintz-covered armchairs, Rachel tried to compose her mind for the coming experience. After a moment, she got up again to go and unlock a drawer in the fine old desk by the window, and take out the copy of the will which Charles's solicitor had left with her for the purpose. He had offered to relate the relevant detail to Craig Lindhurst himself, but Rachel had felt it incumbent on her to be the one to bear the brunt of that individual's response. They had six months left in which to fulfil the terms; she doubted if six years would make any difference to the way she felt.

Craig arrived at the same time as the tea. He held open the door for the young maid wheeling the trolley, taking it from her with a smile and a word of thanks.

A definite conquest there, judged Rachel, viewing the girl's expression as she turned to go. Dressed now in pale grey trousers and fine-knit white sweater, he was enough, she supposed, to turn any female head. He had even found time for a shave.

'Milk and sugar?' she enquired as he took a seat on the sofa opposite.

'Neither,' he said. 'I like both tea and coffee black and unsweetened.'

'I'll try to remember.' Rachel made no attempt to iron out the acerbic note in her voice. 'How about a sandwich? Smoked salmon, I think.'

'Fine. I didn't get much in the way of lunch.' He helped himself to three of the delicate preparations, sitting back with plate in hand to take down the first in a couple of bites. 'Tasty,' he declared, 'though hardly man-size. I'll need to accustom myself to the refinements of country living.'

Rachel said quickly, 'You do plan on staying, then?'

Grey eyes lifted to regard her with unreadable expression. 'You weren't expecting me to?'

'I wasn't sure what to expect,' she confessed, already regretting the over-hasty remark. 'You don't seem to spend too much time in any one place.'

'I go wherever and whenever the circumstances call for it,' he told her. 'At present I'm contemplating taking a sabbatical in order to write a book.'

'An autobiography?'

The strong mouth took on a slant. 'I've hardly lived long enough yet for that. Not that experience won't provide useful material for the novel I have in mind.'

'War intermingled with sex, I suppose? It's usually a successful formula.'

One dark brow lifted. 'Not the kind of reading I'd have had you down for. Just goes to show how unreliable first impressions can be.'

'Doesn't it?' Rachel refused to allow herself to be in any way thrown by the counter attack. 'You took it for granted I was nothing but a gold-digger out for what I could get. I aim to prove you wrong there too.'

His shrug was brief. 'I'm open to conversion.'

Not easily, she thought. Not without total conviction. What real proof could she offer when it came right down to it? All she had was her word. For this man, it wouldn't be enough.

Unimportant, anyway, she told herself firmly. It was the future, not the past, to which she needed to look. Picking up the sheaf of typed pages from the arm of her chair, she held it out to him.

'You'd better read this.'

CHAPTER TWO

CRAIG set down his plate to take the documents from her and open them up. Rachel watched him run his eyes down over the initial and requisite formal statement followed by a series of minor bequests. Nothing there to disturb him. Charles had been generous to those he'd considered deserving cases, but the sums involved scarcely made a dent in the residue of the estate. Page three was the one where trouble began.

She found herself holding her breath as the grey eyes reached the appropriate paragraphs, letting it out again on a silent sigh as his expression underwent a sudden and totally discouraging alteration. The reaction was one she had anticipated, so why this feeling of let-down? A man of superb self-control Craig Lindhurst might be, but even he was incapable of taking this in his stride.

It seemed an age before he looked up. Rachel steeled herself to meet his gaze with a degree of aplomb.

'You're in agreement with all this?' he asked on an odd note.

'To keep Apperknowle intact, yes,' she said. 'If you read on, you'll see what I mean.'

He did so, expression unchanging this time. Rachel could repeat word for word the phrase that meant the most to her: 'Should the condition laid down not be adhered to, the house and land to be sold for development'. That proposed development had been outlined to her as a bid to turn the whole estate into a timeshare concern, with apartment blocks in the grounds and the pool incorporated into a leisure complex. Over her dead body, had been her immediate reaction.

Charles had known how she would feel about it, of course. The verbal promise he had extracted from her shortly before his death had been by way of a rider to the clause. So far as Rachel herself was concerned, it would have been enough on its own to ensure her co-operation.

'I see you don't go away empty-handed whatever,' Craig commented at length. 'A life income isn't to be sneezed at, even if you wouldn't be able to get your hands on the capital.'

'I'm not interested in the money,' she denied without heat. 'Only in keeping Apperknowle intact.'

'I'd have said the two were synonymous.'

Rachel drew in a long, slow breath. This was proving even more difficult than she had thought. Craig wasn't giving her any leeway at all. 'In a way, they have to be, only that still doesn't mean I'm what you're thinking I am. I made Charles a promise. I intend doing everything I can to keep it.'

'Including marrying a man you don't even know?'

'Yes.' The word came out flat and unemotional.

'I see.' He was looking at her as if he had never seen anything quite like her before, a grim little smile playing about his mouth. 'I'm sure I don't need to point out what else would be expected of us as the next link in the chain? You've obviously covered every aspect.'

A tremor ran through her as she looked into the lean, hard features. When she spoke it was with reserve. 'I'm prepared to further the line, yes.'

Mockery sprang in the grey eyes. 'A delicate way of putting it. Assuming Charles made every attempt to impregnate you while he was alive, what makes you sure the failure wasn't yours to start with?'

Rachel flushed. It took every ounce of control she had to keep her tone from reflecting her thoughts. 'I can't be one hundred per cent sure.'

'But the odds are against it, I agree.' He slid a deliberated glance over the length of her where she såt, taking full stock of the full, firm curves of her breasts beneath the mulberry silk shirt, of the slender length of her legs encased in sheer dark nylon. 'Not a task I'd find exactly onerous myself, I have to admit. You have everything it takes to put a man in the mood.' He gave her no time to form a retort to that remark. 'If this marriage was intended simply for the purpose of securing the line, I don't suppose there'd be any reason why we shouldn't live separate lives otherwise? Or even divorce after the feat was accomplished, if it comes to that?'

Rachel gazed at him in swift and sudden contempt. 'Legally, I don't suppose there is. Considering which, it shouldn't be too difficult a decision to make. After all, if you refuse out of hand, you get peanuts!'

'So I understand.' The asperity had brought a glint to his eyes. 'Charles left little room for manoeuvre.'

Rachel said thickly, 'You mean you accept?'

Craig's laugh was entirely devoid of humour. 'Certainly I accept. I'd be the biggest fool alive to turn down such a tempting offer. How soon can we arrange things?'

Rachel's heart jerked painfully. 'It doesn't have to be immediate. We still have six months before the deadline.'

Broad shoulders lifted in a brief shrug. 'I see no point in waiting. What has to be done has to be done.' The pause held a certain deliberation. 'Unless you'd prefer some tangible evidence of my ability before you take the plunge?'

More than half set for a lengthy battle in persuasion, Rachel felt totally out of her depth with this too ready agreement. Promise or no promise, she wished Craig would simply go away and leave her alone. The very notion of what he was suggesting made her stomach turn over. Were all men as blasé about the sex act as this? she wondered fleetingly. Even without love, there surely had to be a little finesse attached?

'I'm more than willing to wait until after the marriage,' she said stiffly. 'And I'm not prepared to enter into that until Charles has been gone the full year.'

'Because of what people might think?' Craig shook his head. 'Scarcely matters, surely? It couldn't possibly cause more talk than yours and Charles's marriage did.'

'You didn't even come to the wedding,' she challenged. 'How could you know what kind of reaction there was?'

'When winter weds spring the reverberations are felt far and wide.'

'How very poetic!' Her voice was honey-sweet. 'I shouldn't have thought you had it in you to use such phraseology.'

'I have it in me,' he said softly, 'to do all manner of things.'

He got to his feet, ignoring the sheaf of papers which fell to the floor. Rachel sat like a statue as he came round the trolley to reach her. She couldn't even find the will to resist as he drew her up to him. The power she had sensed was there in the strength of the arms he slid around her, in the ruthless quest of the mouth seeking hers.

Charles's kisses had always been so tender, so loving, so infinitely caring. This was like nothing she had ever experienced before—a searching, burning, knee-weakening pressure that caused her lips to flutter open in involuntary response, her whole body to tense against him. She felt the hardness of his chest crushing her breasts, the steely strength of his thigh muscles and undoubtable evidence of his masculinity. Something stirred to life deep down in the very pit of her stomach, curling tendrils of heated sensation through her.

She was too shaken to make a murmur when he put her away from him. All she could do was gaze at him in stunned silence. There was an odd expression in the grey eyes, a certain roughness in his voice when he spoke.

'As I said, everything it takes. I can't blame Charles too much for taking advantage.'

'He didn't,' Rachel protested, finding her voice again, albeit shakily. 'I told you, I loved him. I would never have married him otherwise.'

'I only have your word for that,' he said. 'Irrelevant, anyway, at present.' He paused, eyes veiled again. 'About this marriage...'

'I won't have it too soon.' Rachel tried to infuse certitude into her voice. 'My mother...'

'Would think even worse of you than she already does?' Craig finished for her as she allowed the words to trail away. 'I don't suppose for a moment that you've told your parents exactly what the will says?'

'No, I haven't. And it's only the one parent. My father died seven years ago.'

His expression altered a little. 'That might explain a whole lot.'

Her head came up. 'If you're thinking what I think you are, forget it. I loved Charles as a man, not a substitute!'

'You think you'd have loved him as well as you did if he'd been poor?'

'Whatever.'

Craig shook his head and turned away, going back to regain his seat and the uneaten sandwiches, and leaving her with no recourse but to sink back into her own seat in contemplation of a cup of tea gone stone-cold.

'I'll pour some fresh,' she said, reaching for the other cup. She slung the cold black dregs into the receptacle provided, refilled from the silver pot, and handed the cup back again before repeating the action for herself. Playing for time, she knew. Nothing was going quite the way she had anticipated. Craig had little call to regard her as a gold-digger when he was willing to go so far himself for mere monetary gain.

'So what would you suggest we do with the time between now and the marriage?' he asked.

'You said you were planning on writing a book,' she rejoined. 'What better place than this to take your sabbatical?'

'Live and work here for the next six months? Won't that in itself cause the talk you're so afraid of?'

Rachel ignored the irony. 'It might if it were just the two of us alone. With Mrs Brantley here too, the situation is rather different. Now that things are ... resolved between us, it can become common knowledge that you inherited half the estate. So far only myself and Charles's solicitor—Julian Turnbull—know.'

The mobile left eyebrow quirked again. 'That's going to be something of a shock for your mother too, isn't it? How do you intend explaining the delay in informing her that you're not sole beneficiary?'

'Simply enough. The detail had to be kept secret until you'd been contacted. Julian will back me on that score.' Rachel added curiously, 'Where exactly were you all these months, anyway? It was as if you'd dropped off the face of the earth!'

The firm mouth acquired a suddenly thinner line. 'Doing my job in circumstances I'd as soon not go into. I'm here now. That's all that need concern you.'

'Sorry I asked.' She had bridled afresh at his tone. 'Far be it from me to pry into your affairs!'

'Temper,' he remonstrated, regaining his former mocking mien. 'If we're going to play this thing the way you want it played, we'll need to appear compatible— on the surface, at least. That's assuming you do want people to think we're marrying for love and not just convenience?'

Rachel bit her lip. The taunt hurt no less for its being on line. She couldn't bear for anyone else to know the truth. Pretending to fall in love with this man she was coming closer to detesting, at the moment, was not going to be any easy part to play. Yet play it she must. For her mother's sake as well as her own.

'You still didn't say whether you were going to stay on,' she said on an unemotional note. 'There's everything here you'd need—including Charles's study to work in if you like.'

'Yes, I am,' he returned equably. 'I can't think of a better venue either. I'll sublet the flat for the time being.'

'Are you really going to need it again at all, considering?' she queried, and elicited a brief shrug.

'Quite apart from the fact that it's always useful to have a place up in town, you don't imagine I'll be retiring here on the strength of my half-share in all this, do you? A few months working on the book I can stand. Any longer would drive me out of my mind with boredom. What the devil do you find to do with your days on an island twelve by twenty-one?'

'Plenty,' Rachel said. 'I've never been bored in my life!' She added with purpose, 'I always think it shows a lack of imagination.'

'You're probably right,' Craig agreed imperturbably. 'I'm all for action myself.'

'Which doesn't say much for the novel you're planning to write. Imagination surely has to play a part in any fictional account?'

Craig's laugh held genuine amusement. 'Quick off the mark, aren't you? If I do get stuck for ideas I'll know where to turn.' He paused, eyeing her thoughtfully. 'You were Charles's secretary before you married, weren't you? Good typist?'

'Of course.' Rachel's mind had already leapt ahead. 'I'd be willing to help out in any way, if that's what you're going to ask.'

'Could be. My typing is strictly of the two-fingered variety—fast, but not particularly accurate. Of no account when I'm phoning copy through, but a manuscript needs to be presented properly.'

'You have a publisher already in mind?'

'And interested. One of the perks of knowing the right people. It will be faction, by the way, not wholly fiction. You might find some of the background detail upsetting.'

'I dare say I can weather it.' Rachel was taken by the idea to the point where she could almost forget the main reason he was going to be here at all. 'When were you thinking of making a start?'

'The sooner the better. I'd need to go back up to town to arrange things, naturally, but that should only take a day or two.'

'You'd be leaving straight away, then?'

The smile held derision. 'Say Monday. That gives us the weekend. You'll need to introduce me to your mother, among others. Whereabouts on the island does she live?'

'Over Sandown way.' It was all going too fast for Rachel's taste; Craig appeared to be taking over. 'It can wait until you get back.'

'I don't think so.' His tone was easy enough, but there was a look in the grey eyes that challenged her to argue further. 'Putting things off isn't my style. I'd suggest dinner tonight, right here. That way we get it over and done with early doors. I can break the news to my mother when I see her.'

Rachel bit back on the instinctive comment. Somehow it hadn't occurred to her that his mother might also still be around. Unless she'd had her first child latish on in life, she probably wouldn't be all that much older than her own surviving parent. Not that it was likely the two of them would have anything in common.

'I'll have to see whether she's free tonight,' she hedged.

'So do it now,' he returned, with obviously no intention of letting her off the hook. 'There's a telephone right over there on the desk.'

Rachel found herself on her feet and responding to the command almost like an automaton. This was crazy, she fumed. He had only been here five minutes! All the same, having begun to obey, she could hardly turn tail now. A part of her had to concede that he was right, too. Her mother deserved to know what was going on, if only up to a point.

Laura Howard ran a small arts and crafts shop to which she contributed a number of home-made but by no means amateurishly executed items herself. It was her present plan to buy up the premises shortly to become vacant next door, and extend the business into a cottage tea-rooms. As a mainly seasonal venture, the project had engendered little enthusiasm with her bank. Now that her own financial future was resolved, Rachel thought as she dialled the number, she would be in a position to offer assistance. Whether it would be accepted was something else again.

It was almost a full minute before Laura answered the call. 'Merlin's Cave,' she announced. 'Sorry for the delay. I had a customer. How can I help you?'

Conscious of Craig listening from a few feet away, Rachel tried to keep her tone casual. 'Mom, it's me. Are you free to come over to dinner tonight?'

'Well...yes, I suppose so,' came the answer on a note of faint surprise. 'Why such short notice?'

'There's someone I'd like you to meet.' She tagged on impulsively, 'And something I couldn't tell you before that I need to explain about.'

There was a lengthy pause before Laura responded. She sounded reticent. 'Nice or not so nice?'

'It depends on your viewpoint.' Rachel couldn't bring herself to say any more than that. 'Shall I send the car to pick you up?'

The reply was not unanticipated. 'No, thanks, I'll drive myself over. Seven-thirty all right?'

'Fine. See you later, then. Bye for now.'

'I gather she doesn't go a bundle on the idea of being chauffeured?' commented Craig as Rachel replaced the receiver. 'Can't say I blame her.'

Doing a swift review of the only end of the conversation he could have heard, she said caustically, 'What gives you that impression?'

'Your tone of voice. You sounded resigned.' He twisted in his seat to look at her as she stood there by the desk.

'If you already knew how she was likely to respond, why make the offer in the first place?'

'Because there's always the chance that she may decide to take advantage. I suppose you're another who finds Grayson unnecessary?'

'As one who also prefers to drive himself, yes. I'd have thought you'd prefer your independence too.'

'I don't drive,' she said.

'Don't?' he queried. 'Or can't?'

'Can't, then.' She lifted her shoulders. 'I never got round to learning.'

'Then it's high time you did. We'll make it a priority once I'm here.'

'You'll be too busy writing your book,' she came back hastily, and saw his mouth take on the fast-becoming-familiar slant.

'I don't propose teaching you myself. That would put paid to any chance we might have of achieving a steady relationship. I'm sure there are plenty of good driving schools on the island.'

Rachel's knuckles were white where she gripped the desk-edge. 'Don't try to run my life for me!' she snapped. 'I'm more than capable of making my own decisions! I'll learn to drive when I'm good and ready, not before.'

The shrug suggested a certain indifference. 'Just a thought. Far be it from me to try forcing you into anything you don't want to do.'

It was on the tip of Rachel's tongue to apologise for the display of petulance, but something in her wouldn't allow the words to pass her lips. To marry a man who could elicit the kind of aggression seething within her would be the act of an idiot; yet what other choice did she have, short of denying Charles his last request? She was trapped, and had to make the best of things. Only that didn't have to include kowtowing to Craig Lindhurst!

'I think I'll take myself on a walk around the gardens,' he said now, getting to his feet again. 'Give the two of us time to recoup for the evening. It wouldn't do for your mother to see us at loggerheads, if she's to be convinced of the mutual attraction scheduled to develop into a marrying emotion over the next few weeks, would it?'

Rachel stayed where she was as he left the room. She felt completely at sea. The kiss Craig had pressed on her was still imprinted on her lips, the lean, hard strength of his body a memory she couldn't close out. There would be no need to fake the physical attraction because it was right there in her, hate to admit it though she might. Craig Lindhurst was no gentleman in the way Charles had been, but he set up a need in her that had nothing to do with gentleness and courtesy. It was that which she had to fight.

She saw nothing of him over the following couple of hours. At seven-twenty, dressed in dark blue silk jersey, she went down to the drawing-room to be on hand when her mother arrived. A gin and tonic helped calm her nerves a little. Once through the initial introduction and announcement, she would be all right.

The room itself was some help. Decorated in shades of peach and white, with lovely antique pieces mingled with the comparatively new in furnishings, it radiated a warmth and comfort that belied its size.

As in all the downstairs rooms—and some of those on the upper floor too—there was a fireplace, in this case a genuine Adam. Standing before it, Rachel gazed longingly at the framed photograph of her and Charles, taken on their wedding day. If only he were still here she would be so happy. Why, oh, why had he had to go?

Craig still hadn't put in an appearance when her parent arrived. Naturally blonde like herself, and wearing a purple culotte suit, Laura Howard at forty-eight was no middle-aged mother figure. Losing her husband at such an early age had placed her in a position where she had been forced either to remodel her life completely or simply stagnate. She led a full social life, and seemed content enough on the surface, although Rachel often wondered if she really was satisfied with the way things were. Widowhood was a lonely affair, no matter what the consolations; she herself could vouch for that.

'So where is this person you want me to meet?' was the first question put after greetings were exchanged.

'He'll be down any time,' Rachel replied, and saw the blue eyes so like her own cool a little.

'A man? Staying here?'

Rachel drew in a steadying breath before launching into explanations, angry that Craig wasn't here himself to help out, although what contribution he might have made she wasn't at all sure. Laura listened without comment right through to the final stumbling, 'So you see, I couldn't tell you before.'

'I fail to see why exactly,' Laura said. 'But mine's not the right to question. Does this...Craig, did you say...intend living at Apperknowle long term?'

'He'll be here for some months at least,' Rachel replied, sticking to the truth as far as she was able. 'He's planning on writing a novel here.'

Some flicker of unreadable expression crossed the older woman's still attractive features. 'Really? Is he an established author?'

'Not yet, but aiming to be,' said the subject under discussion from the doorway.

He advanced into the room, his frank appraisal totally without self-consciousness. He was wearing a grey suit of the same steely shade as his eyes, along with a pristine white shirt and a navy and grey striped tie. The latter two items were silk, Rachel was sure. Obviously not a man who skimped on personal expenditure. Taken along with the Jaguar at present undergoing repair, and the London flat, it was becoming apparent that he wasn't exactly lacking in finances already, which made his over-hasty acceptance of Charles's decree even more reprehensible.

'Rachel will have told you the facts by now, I imagine?' he said to Laura as the two of them shook hands. 'I thought I'd give the two of you a few minutes on your own for the purpose. It came as quite a shock to me too, so you don't need to put up any pretence.'

'I wasn't about to,' Laura acknowledged. 'Charles was perfectly entitled to do whatever he thought fit with his property. Half of everything still leaves Rachel in a position where she needs to keep an eye open for opportunists from now on.'

'Drink?' asked Rachel hastily, avoiding Craig's glance. 'Your usual sherry, Mom?'

'Let me get them,' said Craig. 'Just point me in the right direction.'

Rachel ceded with good grace. 'The lacquered cabinet over there. I'll have another G and T, please.'

He took the glass from her, and crossed to the cabinet, pulling down the front flap to reveal the array of bottles and glasses and decanters. Laura watched him for a moment, then turned her attention back to her daughter.

'Different from what I expected,' she said *sotto voce*.

Different from what *she* had expected, Rachel could have told her. The masculine attraction Craig exuded might make the duties she would be called on to perform somewhat less onerous than they might have been, but it would still be a basic biological function when it boiled down to it.

Considering the circumstances, the evening, she supposed, was a success. Craig and her mother seemed to get along fine once the initial reserve had worn off. Reserve only on her mother's part, at that, Rachel was bound to acknowledge. Craig was at ease from the first.

Laura left at ten-thirty, pleading an early start at the shop. Saturday was her busiest time. Rachel went out to see her off.

'I like him,' declared her mother. 'I think he could be a bit of a ruthless character where the occasion called for it, but then, he'd need to be in his line of work.' She eyed her daughter reflectively. 'You might have problems when it comes to any major decisions regarding Apperknowle.'

'It can't be sold,' Rachel responded. 'Not unless...' she caught herself up, biting her lip, then tagged on quickly '...unless he had the will overruled in court.'

'In which case he could well finish up with less than he started, depending on the judge's leanings. Not a risk I see him taking.' She slid behind the wheel of the blue Sierra, and closed the door, winding down the window to add, 'Don't forget the craft fair in a couple of weeks. I'm relying on you for help with my stall.'

'I won't,' Rachel promised. 'I'll see you before then, anyway. Goodnight, Mom.'

She watched her mother drive out of sight before turning to go back indoors. The night air felt cool on her skin. She was glad of the warmth to be found inside. Craig had stayed in the drawing-room. He was lounging

comfortably on one of the brocade sofas set at right
angles to the fireplace when she returned to the room.

'Nice woman,' he commented. 'Intelligent too.'

'Not what you expected, perhaps?' Rachel queried
shortly.

He shook his head, unmoved by her tone. 'I try to
keep an open mind.'

'Not where I'm concerned, it seems. You still believe
I only married Charles for what I could get out of him,
don't you?'

He regarded her steadily. 'I'm willing to be convinced. If Charles really meant so much to you, you'd
be rather more eager than you are to fulfil his last wishes.
He's already been dead six months. Why wait another
six? People are still going to talk, whatever.'

'Not as much as they would if the marriage was to
take place as soon as you're intimating,' she snapped
back. 'It's going to be difficult enough to go through
with at all, without making it even worse! Unfortunately
I can't claim the same clinical outlook when it comes
to...' She sought for words, aware of his sardonic smile
at her hesitation.

'When it comes to performing the necessary function,
is what I think you're trying to say. For the record, my
outlook regarding lovemaking is far from clinical.
Mutual enjoyment would be closer to the mark.'

'A subject I'm sure you know all there is to know
about,' Rachel responded tautly. 'Except that I happen
to consider the word "love" misplaced in that context.
Lustmaking might be closer to the mark!'

'A matter of interpretation. Two people don't have to
be in love to enjoy the physical expression.' He studied
her thoughtfully for a moment, taking in the flush high-
lighting her cheekbones. 'So maybe I was wrong about

your motives in marrying Charles. Maybe you really did love him in your own way. You give a surface impression of maturity, but underneath you're still a rather naïve little girl. It's time you grew up, Rachel. Time you learned a few facts of life.'

'If that means acquiring the kind of cynicism you've developed, I'll not bother, thanks.' Her tone would have cut glass. 'Supposing we call this conversation closed?'

'What exactly are you most afraid of?' he mocked. 'Or should I say who?'

'Whom?' she corrected with deliberation. 'And it isn't fear I'm feeling so much as revulsion. If Charles had known you better, I'm sure he'd never have asked it of me!'

'Fear I said and fear I meant,' came the calm insistence. 'The response I roused in you earlier shook you to the core, didn't it? You'd never known it could be like that—especially with a man you don't even like, much less love.'

Rachel's nails were cutting into the palms of her hands. Her voice sounded thick. 'You took me by surprise, that's all.'

Craig laughed. 'Perhaps I should have done just that. If so, you might be feeling quite differently about everything by now. Deny it all you like but there's a real live woman in there somewhere. One quite capable of giving back as good as she gets. Charles might have treated you like Dresden china, but I've no such intention.'

'Go to hell!' she said with force.

For a brief moment his expression sobered. 'I've been.' He lightened his tone again, his smile mocking her impotent anger. 'Don't take life so seriously. There's still fun to be had if you look for it.'

'Not your kind.' She regained control of herself with an effort, aware of the trembling in her limbs. 'You've been here only a matter of hours and already everything's falling apart. I'm not sure even Apperknowle is worth it any more!'

'But your word to Charles surely is—unless you're changing your mind about that too?'

'No. No, of course not.' She gave a shuddering half-sob. 'Just back off, will you? Give me time.'

'I'll think about it.' He hauled himself to his feet, shaking his head as she took an involuntary backward step. 'Don't concern yourself. Right now I'm too bone-weary to do either of us justice. I didn't get much sleep on the plane last night. We've the whole weekend ahead. Time enough for anything. Are you ready to go up too?'

Rachel shook her head, not trusting her voice.

'Then I'll say goodnight,' he said. 'Watch out for the bedbugs.'

She sank nervelessly to a seat in the nearest chair as the door closed behind him. Craig was right about one thing: she was afraid. The fear had begun this afternoon when he had kissed her and the world had spun about her head. She wanted it to happen again, and she mustn't. It was a betrayal of her love for Charles. All she needed from Craig was a child with a right to the name of Lindhurst. After that he could go his own way.

CHAPTER THREE

WAKING in the bedroom she had shared with Charles normally gave Rachel a pang or two. This particular Saturday morning her first thought was of the man who was to become her next husband. The early sunlight slanting in through the windows went some way towards dispelling the pessimism she felt. On such a day it was difficult to be totally gloomy in outlook.

Also boasting a four-poster bed, the room was large enough to have a sitting area too. Rachel had herself chosen the colour scheme of pale green, pink and white, extending it out on to the covered balcony with its cushioned wrought-iron chairs and table. She drew on the wrap which matched her pink satin nightdress before going out to lean on the balustrade and draw in deep breaths of the fresh and fragrant air. There was nothing anywhere to beat this!

Below and beyond the rear terrace lay the pool. Scorning the normal oblong, Charles had opted for an elliptical shape set within a broad patio, around which were planted shrubs and small trees to create a certain privacy. From where she stood, Rachel could see over the latter to the calm blue water. Even as she looked, that calm was shattered by the impact of some diving body.

Using a strong crawl, Craig completed several lengths before finally hoisting himself out to sit on the edge of the pool and run a hand over his hair to squeeze out excess moisture. His body was tanned the colour of teak, his chest broad and powerful beneath its light coating of hair. Even sitting the way he was, there was no sagging of stomach muscle over the band of the blue trunks—no hint of surplus flesh anywhere on the finely toned body.

Rachel registered that fact with a tensing of her own stomach muscles. Charles had been in good physical shape for his age, but there had been no disguising a certain coarsening of skin and greying of body hair. She had not found it off-putting then, and didn't find the memory so now, but neither could she deny the superior quality of fit and healthy youth. Craig was a magnificent specimen of the male. She would have to be blind and insensible not to acknowledge it.

As if registering her observation, he looked in the direction of the house, lifting a hand in greeting when he saw her standing there.

'Come on down,' he called. 'The water's fine!'

The pool had only been refilled a week or so ago, and so far Rachel had been in no more than a couple of times. She had no intention now of responding to the invitation. Something in her fought shy of revealing herself to him in a swimsuit at this stage. Ridiculous, she knew, considering what was eventually to take place between them, but that was in a future far enough away at present to be disregarded.

She turned back into the room without acknowledging him. There were two whole days to get through before she gained the breathing-space she so badly needed. Two days, and two nights. Sleep hadn't come easily last night. She had lain restless for what seemed like hours before finally dropping into a fitful doze. Yet she didn't feel so much tired at the moment as jittery. Every nerve in her body seemed to be on edge.

Breakfast was served, as always, in the morning-room. Seeing the table laid for two again after so many lonely months brought mingled emotions. Nice to have company while one ate, but better if it were anyone else but Craig. She didn't feel up to facing him just yet.

He arrived along with the coffee. In fact, he brought it in with him, having met up with Doreen, the maid, in the hall.

'Lovely morning,' he observed as he helped himself to cereal from the assortment on offer. 'You should have come for a swim. It's a great way to start the day.'

'Too cool for me out there as yet,' Rachel excused herself. 'Perhaps in a week or two.'

He gave her a derisive look. 'So why have the pool filled at all if you weren't planning on using it yet?'

'I meant in the early morning,' she said. 'Not the whole day.'

'In that case, we'll take a bathe together this afternoon. Which leaves us with the morning to fill in. Any suggestions?'

Rachel lifted her shoulders. 'A drive round the island, perhaps, if you haven't seen it in ten years?'

'I can't say I saw all that much of it even then,' he admitted. 'OK, you're on. Providing I do the driving, that is. I imagine Charles didn't rely wholly on the Rolls for transport?'

'No,' she admitted with reluctance. 'There's a Mercedes coupé in the garage.'

'That's a bit more like it.' He cocked a glance. 'You'd find it an easy enough drive yourself. Smooth as silk gearbox.'

'If I learn to drive at all it will be in an automatic,' she retorted.

'You have to be able to handle a manually geared car in order to take your test,' came the prompt return.

'Then I shan't bother. I'm not mechanically minded.'

'Pig-headed is the word I'd use.'

'That's two words,' she said pedantically.

'Hyphenated.' He was beginning to sound just a mite impatient. 'You're determined to make this whole affair as difficult as possible for us both, aren't you? Does that salve your conscience in any way?'

Her head jerked upright. '*I* don't have a conscience to salve!'

'But you think I should have, is that it?' His lips had thinned. 'Where would it have left you if I'd turned the whole idea down? Unless, of course, you've decided that death-bed promises are non-binding after all?'

'It wasn't like that,' Rachel denied. 'He didn't——'

'You both knew he was dying,' he cut in, correctly surmising what she was about to say. 'It scarcely matters at just what point he extracted the promise. He had no right to ask it of you.' His tone roughened a little. 'If it comes to that, he'd no right to talk you into marrying him in the first place!'

'He didn't talk me into it,' she said between her teeth. 'He asked.'

'Making it just about impossible for you to say no by playing on your sensibilities.'

'No!' Rachel was breathing hard, hanging on to her temper by a thread. 'Only last night you were still more than half convinced that I was the advantage-taker.'

'So I changed my mind. I don't mind admitting to being wrong on occasion.' Craig studied her stormy eyes, his own impenetrable. 'Unless we actually contest the will in open court, the marriage has to take place—if you want to keep Apperknowle intact, that is—but there was nothing said about children. Did your promise to Charles actually go that far?'

'Yes, it did. What would be the point in keeping Apperknowle intact if there were no heir to take over?' Rachel was doing her best to retain control. 'Do you really think I'd even consider marrying you if there were any way out of it?'

'There is,' Craig returned levelly. 'All you have to do is say the word. You'd still have six months to find somewhere else to live. With the kind of income you'd have, that shouldn't be too difficult.'

She gazed at him in sudden confusion. 'That would leave you with nothing.'

'It isn't me we're talking about,' he said. 'It's you.' He paused, watching the conflicting expressions chasing across her face while still revealing nothing of what was going on in his own head. 'Is it worth it?'

There was a kind of desperation in her answer. 'I gave my word.'

His shrug was brief and dismissive. 'So be it. But if we're going to play this game, we play it my way.' He gave her no time to form an answer. 'I'll need to contact my insurance company before they close for the weekend. I'd also like to get some idea of how the place is organised, so we'll put off the island tour for the time being. There's an estate manager, I believe?'

Rachel nodded, hardly trusting her voice.

'And where might he be found on a Saturday morning?'

'At home,' she said. 'He doesn't work weekends unless there's something pressing crops up.'

'It just did. Where does he work from when he's here?'

'The estate office is down by the old stables.'

Rachel could see nothing to be gained from arguing the toss on this subject. As half-owner, Craig had a perfect right to demand to be put in the picture. Robert Wallace, the manager, wasn't going to be too pleased to have his weekend disrupted, but that wasn't her concern. Since Charles's death, she had taken little real interest in the running of the estate as such. If it came right down to it, she acknowledged in a sudden burst of honesty, she had taken little real interest in anything very much these last months. It was high time she kicked herself back into touch.

The rugby term springing instinctively to mind brought a wry smile to her lips. Her father had been a keen amateur player in his time. He would have been in complete agreement with Craig, and just about everyone else, regarding her marriage with Charles. She was the only one who would ever know how truly happy they had been together that brief year.

Craig ate a full cooked breakfast while she toyed with toast and scrambled egg. Fresh coffee was brought, poured and drunk, and the table finally vacated around nine o'clock. Weekdays, Rachel was normally finished by eight-thirty at the latest, giving her time and to spare for anything she felt like doing with her day. The thought of getting back to work when Craig began this book was good. She had insisted on retaining her scarcely over-demanding secretarial position with Charles even after the wedding, but it was some time now since she had last touched a typewriter-keyboard. Fortunately, like riding a bicycle, it was an art which, once learned, was never forgotten, although she might be a little rusty when it came to speed, she supposed.

She showed Craig where the study was, so that he could telephone his insurance company in privacy. The car must have been garaged while he was abroad, she guessed—unless he had loaned it to someone. Closing the door on him, she stood for a moment going over all that had been said at the breakfast table, dwelling in particular on that final statement of intent. They would not be playing things his way, she told herself emphatically. Not while she had anything at all to do with it. Six months—no more, no less. By that time she might have found some form of reconciliation.

She spent the morning sorting out some items for the local village jumble sale. All of Charles's things had gone to Oxfam, packed up by Mrs Brantley, as Rachel had been unable to bring herself to perform the task. The huge wardrobes lining the dressing-room were relatively empty these days. Clothes had never been her overriding interest. Charles himself had not been socially active since his illness had struck him down, so there had been little need for new ones. Most of what she had were left-overs from her 'single' days.

It was really time she began thinking of replenishing, she thought now, if only as a tribute of a kind to Charles himself. There were plenty of boutiques in Newport, although a trip across to Southampton might provide more scope. London was the best place of all, of course, but if she did go there it would have to be at a time when Craig wasn't.

Everything hinged on that individual, she reflected wryly. It was the male side of any union that supposedly governed the sex of a child. Supposing it turned out to be a girl—a factor Charles didn't appear to have taken into consideration? In which case, she supposed, they would simply have to try again—and keep on trying until they succeeded. Always providing that Craig himself proved willing to stay the course.

Lunchtime was on her before she realised. She had ordered cold salmon and salad, followed by lemon meringue, and could only hope that it would be enough for a man of Craig's undoubted appetite. Charles had eaten sparingly himself.

Craig was emerging from his room further along the galleried landing when she went out. He had changed from the jeans and sweater in which he had begun the day into beige trousers and cotton shirt. Dressed in the same cream skirt and blouse she had worn at breakfast, Rachel felt self-conscious.

'How did it go?' she asked. 'With Robert, I mean.'

'Fair enough,' he acknowledged. 'On the face of it, the place is well run. The farms don't bring in much of a profit, but I suppose that's only to be expected under the present climate. Did Charles never consider leasing out that parcel of land on the cliff-top as a caravan park?'

'No, he didn't!' The denial was sharp. 'And I hope you're not considering it either. That would be almost as bad as letting the whole estate go for development!'

'Just an idea. If you're against it, I obviously can't do much about it. Wallace seems to share your outlook.'

'He's an island man born and bred, and hates the way tourism is taking over. We're not exactly living on the breadline, anyway, so why this urge to capitalise?'

The smile was fleeting. 'Shades of my brother in me, I expect. Forget it.'

They had reached the head of the stairs. Beginning to descend, Rachel caught the heel of her shoe on the edge of the tread, and would have fallen headlong if Craig hadn't grabbed her arm. Hauled upright, she found herself close up against the lean, hard body in a manner too reminiscent of the previous day's experience. The tremor which ran through her was the product of an emotion that had little to do with her near-accident.

'You need to look where you're going,' he said softly. 'That could have been a nasty tumble.'

'Just a slip. I'm all right now, thanks.' She made to draw away. 'Really.'

'Your heart's going like a trip-hammer,' he observed, making no attempt to release her. 'I can hear it from here.'

There was every chance that he was speaking the truth; her heartbeats sounded like thunder in her own ears. She tried to pass the moment off with a shaky laugh. 'Don't exaggerate. It wasn't that close a shave.'

The grey eyes were shrewd as they rested on her flushed face. 'It could have been. High heels may enhance the female leg, but they're lethal when it comes to retaining balance. I'd advise flatties for everyday wear.'

The fact that she would normally be wearing, if not exactly flatties, certainly a much lower heel than the ones she had on now brought more warmth to Rachel's cheeks. The added height gave her a kind of added assurance—badly needed in any dealings with this man who was all too soon to be her husband. Not that the extra three inches brought her on a level. His mouth was directly in her line of sight.

The tip of her tongue came out to dampen lips gone suddenly dry. She saw a muscle jerk along his jawline, and felt the hands still holding her tauten their grasp. This time she fought the kiss, jerking back from him as if she had been stung, her whole body rigid. 'Don't!'

Craig studied her with a look almost of amusement on his face. 'Why the reticence? We're going to be doing a lot more than just kissing when the time comes.'

'But that isn't yet, and I don't want you touching me in the meantime,' she got out, and saw the smile in his eyes become a spark.

'Well, that's too bad because I'm not cold-blooded enough simply to perform the act without any build-up. You won't be letting Charles down by allowing yourself to enjoy it.'

He was too shrewd by half, Rachel acknowledged. He was all too well aware of the feelings he elicited in her. But it wasn't only Charles she felt she was letting down; it was herself too. Feeling anything at all for a man who was virtually a stranger to her was totally wrong.

'Don't worry about it,' he advised. 'Just let it happen.'

She turned from him blindly, and was halfway down the stairs before she realised it. Craig caught her up at the bottom.

'That was foolish,' he said on an intolerant note. 'What did you think I was about to do—take you there and then? I didn't realise how right I was when I said you needed to grow up!'

'As a widow at twenty-three,' she forced out, 'I'd say I'd done my fair share!'

'I'm not talking about grief, and well you know it. Charles might have been ruthless enough to extract that promise from you at a time when he knew you'd refuse him nothing, but even he wouldn't have expected you to fulfil it in cold blood!' Craig was angry now, and making no attempt to disguise it. 'Let yourself start living a little, for God's sake! There's nothing wrong with wanting a man.'

Rachel's laugh was designed to ridicule. 'That's reading rather a lot into a very little, isn't it? Or are you of the opinion that all women want you that way?'

'I've only had dealings with a minority,' came the cool retort, 'so I can't answer for the rest. You've been six months without a man after a year of marriage. It's only natural that you're feeling the loss in all ways, not just the one.'

'Meaning I'd have the hots for any man I came into contact with at present?' she queried bitingly, forgetting her stress in the sudden cold fury of the moment.

Anger gave way to amusement. 'A turn of phrase I'd never have expected from such sweet lips! Encouraging, though, I have to admit.' He added smoothly, 'Not any man—just those with the right credentials.'

'And you consider yourself one of them, of course!'

There were dancing lights in the grey eyes. 'There'll come a time when you'll be in a position to judge for yourself. Until then, you'll need to take my word for it. Shall we go and feed the inner man?'

Short of shunning the luncheon table altogether, there wasn't much else she *could* do, Rachel conceded. She felt torn in two by conflicting emotions. Detest Craig at this moment though she might, she couldn't deny the physical attraction. The next time he attempted to kiss her she doubted if she was going to be strong-minded enough to resist.

They spent the afternoon walking round the estate itself. Reaching the cliff-top pasture to which Craig had referred, Rachel was bound to admit that it would indeed make an ideal caravan site, hidden from the house by a natural fold in the landscape. Not that she had any intention of following through on the idea. Charles had been a shrewd investor; financially, there were no problems. He would have been horrified at the very notion of holiday-makers utilising the land.

It was Craig who suggested they descend the narrow path to the crescent of beach. While not exactly part of the estate, the latter was cut off by the tides to a point where it became almost entirely private. The swimming was safe enough at low tide, but inadvisable when the waves came sweeping in across the flanking points. The water was far too cold as yet anyway, Rachel advised when the subject was raised.

'Something to look forward to in a few weeks, then,' said Craig amicably. 'I understand there's a boat berthed at Cowes. Do you sail?'

'Charles was teaching me,' she admitted. 'He was an expert, of course. He'd taken part in at least a couple of Fastnets, plus other events. And it's actually two boats, not just the one. There's the *Silver Streak* he used for racing, and a dinghy called *Little Streak*, which was just for fun.'

Craig glanced her way. 'You're using the past tense. Does that mean you haven't been out in either of them since Charles died?'

She shook her head. '*Silver Streak* is obviously way outside my league, and I haven't felt like trying the dinghy on my own.' It was her turn to cast a glance. 'Do you sail?'

'I've done some. I wouldn't claim to be as expert as Charles obviously was.' He paused. 'There's not much point in hanging on to the yacht, is there, if we're neither of us interested in competing? What say we put her up for sale, and just keep the dinghy for messing around in?'

'Together?'

'If you like.' His tone was easy.

Rachel wasn't about to commit herself to anything at this stage. Sailing with Charles had been fun; with Craig she might find it anything but. 'I agree about *Silver Streak*,' she said. 'Charles would have hated her to just stand idle. I've already been approached, as a matter of fact, but nothing could be done until you put in an appearance, of course. Julian Turnbull has the details. He suggested coming out Monday morning to discuss things in general.' Her smile was faint. 'After you'd had some time to get over the shock, he said. But if you're not going to be here...'

'We can fit it in before I leave.' Craig bent and picked up a small pebble, sending it skimming flatly over the shallow waves to bounce several times before finally vanishing. 'Why don't you come with me? Meet my mother. We could take in a show while we're there.'

For a brief moment Rachel actually contemplated it. It would be a good opportunity to do some of the shopping she had promised herself. The thought faded as swiftly as it had come. What she needed most was a few days' respite from Craig's disturbing presence, a little time in which to regain some control over her wayward emotions.

'I don't think so, thanks,' she said. 'There'll be time enough to meet her later, when things are more...settled.'

'You mean when she knows the whole story?'

She looked at him sharply. 'You don't really intend telling her all of it, do you?'

He met her gaze without a flicker. 'You'd rather she believed we'd fallen in love?'

'It could have happened that way,' she protested. 'People do.'

'Not without some convincing build-up. We'd need to put on the same act for your mother too. She's no fool.'

'There's time enough.' The desperation was creeping back. 'Why are you trying to rush things, Craig?'

He studied her as she stood there in the afternoon sunlight, blonde hair tousled by the light breeze. 'Because I find any kind of play-acting difficult,' he said at length. 'Because you're a very lovely and desirable young woman, and I want you—the same way you want me.'

Rachel felt her heart give a painful jerk, the muscles of her inner thighs go into involuntary and unwonted spasm. One step would take her into the arms she knew would be ready for her; the temptation was there in her, almost irresistible in its heady demand. She fought it with every ounce of will-power she could bring to bear.

'I told you earlier, you're reading too much into too little, and too soon. There's a world of difference between a kiss and . . . and all the rest.'

'The word is intercourse, if you want to be technical about it. I prefer to call it making love.' His gaze had narrowed to the soft vulnerability of her mouth. 'I want to make love to you, Rachel. I went to sleep last night thinking about you, I woke up this morning thinking about you. It's rapidly becoming a problem.'

Her breathing had roughened, though not from fear. No man had ever spoken to her this way before. Charles's overtures had made her feel all soft and warm inside, not hot and aching the way she was now. There was a drumming in her ears which she recognised as the magnified sound of her own heartbeats, a sense of being outside herself looking in. When she did find her voice it sounded thick and hoarse.

'It's rapidly becoming obvious that you've been too long deprived!'

Just for a moment the grey eyes held a different kind of spark, then it gave way to cynicism. 'You're quite possibly right. Shall we go? It must be getting close to teatime.'

She had done what she had set out to do and cooled his ardour, Rachel reflected dully as he turned away to start back the way they had come, so why this feeling of let-down? Did she really in her heart of hearts want the kind of instant passion he was offering her?

The answer to that was one she didn't care to examine too closely for fear of what she might find out about herself...

CHAPTER FOUR

JULIAN TURNBULL arrived at ten-thirty on the Monday morning. He was in his sixties, and had known Charles most of his life. Whatever his thoughts concerning his contemporary's last will and testament, he had kept them strictly to himself. He continued to do so in facing the newly arrived legatee.

'There's little I can add to what you already know,' he said over coffee in the library. 'All *I* need to know is whether or not the two of you are agreed on the terms of the will?'

We have six months left to make that decision, Rachel was about to say, but Craig forestalled her.

'We're agreed. The only question remaining is as to when the marriage should take place.'

Julian's expression remained impassive. 'A question only the two of you can decide—providing it comes within the twelve months allotted. Do I take it you'll be staying here at Apperknowle, Mr Lindhurst?'

'Initially,' Craig acknowledged. 'I can't vouch for the long term.'

Julian switched a glance in Rachel's direction as if looking for some sign. She met his gaze with an equability she was far from feeling, relieved when he turned his attention back to Craig again. The latter had kept his distance since Saturday afternoon—in spirit, at least. Until this moment she hadn't been entirely sure of just what reply he might have ready for Julian this morning. Neither, she was forced to admit, had she been sure of her own response to whatever decision he did make. She still wasn't.

Stealing a glance at his lean features as he leaned forward to reach for his coffee-cup, Rachel registered the impact on her heart-strings with rueful resignation. There was no denying his physical attraction; in some ways it might have been easier if she hadn't been so aware of it.

Who was she kidding? came the instant retort. Without that attraction this whole affair would have been even more of an abhorrence. She should consider herself fortunate. Craig Lindhurst might not be the kind of partner she would have chosen for herself, had she been given a choice, but he could have been a great deal worse.

As if feeling her appraisal, he looked across at her, one dark brow lifting in the manner she so hated. His declaration on the beach had not been repeated either in word or deed. He had, in fact, acted the perfect gentleman for the rest of the weekend. Meeting the grey eyes now, seeing the derision therein, she realised that he was well aware of the emotional turmoil inside her. A man of his kind would always know when a woman wanted him—and want him she did, despite all her efforts to disregard that need. He was right; she actually missed the physical expression of love—or her body did. With Craig it would be so very different—she knew that already—but a difference that excited something in her never before touched.

She tore her gaze away from his to reach for her own cup with a hand that trembled a little. In a couple of hours he would be gone, though for how long exactly he hadn't said. By the time he returned, she had to be in control of herself to the point where she could at least pretend to view the affair objectively. Craig might well want her, but he felt nothing for her beyond that, nor probably ever would. That was what she had to keep telling herself.

Julian left some short time later. Booked on the one-thirty ferry, Craig was taking the Mercedes in lieu of his own car, which was still undergoing repair. Rachel had ordered lunch for noon in order to give him plenty of time to drive the distance. He had not repeated his invitation to go with him, nor shown any signs of doing so. Not that she would have accepted, in any case.

'That was pretty painless,' he commented at the table. 'I had the feeling there might be a few more surprises in store.'

'Such as?' Rachel queried, and saw the broad shoulders lift.

'Who knows? My uncle was a man of many parts—none of them predictable.'

'Your own viewpoint, or your father's?'

He eyed her assessingly for a moment before answering, his tone surprisingly mild. 'Mostly Dad's, I'd say, considering how little I actually knew your late husband.'

'You visited him ten years ago,' she said. 'There must have been a good reason.'

'There was. It had to do with the fact that my father was going under financially, and, while I wasn't in a position then to help him myself, his brother most certainly was.'

'And did he?'

'Yes. Not that Dad wanted to accept. He'd set out to make it on his own rather than hang around Apperknowle knowing it would never be his. The trouble was, he didn't have the kind of cut-throat attitude needed to stay the pace.'

'So what happened?' she prompted.

'He was killed two months later in a car crash.' Craig said it matter-of-factly. 'Charles was offered repayment out of the estate, but he declined. The upshot was that my mother was left comfortably off. She's editorial director of a publishing company in the city.' He caught the swift change of expression in Rachel's eyes and inclined his head. 'Yes, the same one interested in my book. I don't mind admitting to using her influence. All I need now is the hundred thousand or so words in the right order, plus a degree of hype, and bingo!'

Rachel allowed herself an answering smile. 'You make it sound almost easy. Shall you be doing a synopsis first?'

'It's already done,' he said. 'In my mind, at any rate. I had time on my hands these last months.'

She longed to ask him how and why, but he had turned his attention to the food in front of him with the look of one who had already said more than he had intended. She was going to miss him when he went, she thought suddenly. The house was going to seem empty without him. He had brought her back to life in more ways than one. Even anger was preferable to apathy.

He left for Cowes at one o'clock. Rachel went out to see him off, half hoping and half fearing that he would take it into his head to kiss her goodbye. She was left feeling desolate rather than relieved when he made no attempt to so much as touch her hand. Watching the car disappear down the drive, she wondered hollowly if he had changed his mind about wanting her. All fires needed fuel to keep them glowing, and she had offered little enough encouragement.

The fact that she could be thinking and feeling this way about him at all after such a relatively short time brought a sense of shame. Yet it was better, surely, to have some kind of emotional involvement than to do what had to be done in cold blood? What she had to avoid was any real depth of involvement, because Craig had made it clear that he had no intention of spending the rest of his life at Apperknowle. Once she became pregnant he would have fulfilled his duty.

With a whole afternoon and evening stretching ahead, she found herself cudgelling her mind for some way of passing the time. It was with some reluctance that she finally decided to take Keith Barratt up on his invitation and get in touch with his wife. She and Lindsay had been at school together. Best friends, in fact. True, that friendship had ceased to be quite as close after Lindsay had started going out with Keith at sixteen, but Rachel had still been the one invited to act as chief bridesmaid when the two were married three years ago. They had a little girl of eighteen months now and, from what she had heard, another baby on the way.

Lindsay answered the phone, making no attempt to conceal her surprise at hearing Rachel's voice.

'Keith said you might call, but I didn't really believe you would,' she admitted. 'By all means come on over. Gemma's at my mother's for the afternoon, and Keith's on duty, but I'll be glad to see you.' There was a slight hesitation before she added, 'Only don't bring the Rolls, will you? I'd never hear the last of it from the neighbours.'

'I won't,' Rachel promised, wryly acknowledging that Craig had had a point when he'd said she needed to be able to drive herself. Not that it would have made much difference at present, as he had taken the only other vehicle. Anyway, it wasn't really such a problem, as she could always summon a taxi. 'I'll be there around three,' she said.

The Barratts lived just outside Shanklin on a small estate of modern semis. Lindsay was at the front door when the taxi drew up at five minutes past the hour. Slender of build, she scarcely looked any older than she had the last time Rachel had seen her, her long fair hair tied back from a face that had lost none of its girlish prettiness. So far there was relatively little sign of the new baby, although she had to be a good five months on, Rachel calculated.

Any lingering reserve was dispelled over tea in the comfortable and beautifully decorated living-room. Her attempt to apologise for not getting in touch before was met by a counter apology.

'It was an awkward situation,' Lindsay confessed. 'We weren't sure how to approach it. I mean, marrying a lord, and all that...'

'Especially one old enough to be my grandfather,' Rachel interposed levelly. 'I realise how it must have looked to most people, but I really did love Charles. He was everything a man should be and so rarely is.'

'I'm sure he was.' The other girl hesitated before going on. 'Keith said that one of the men involved in the accident was his nephew?'

'That's right.' Rachel had to fight a sudden urge to let the whole story out of the bag. She settled instead for the same half-truth she had given her mother. 'He and I share the estate.'

Lindsay's eyes widened. 'But I...we thought you'd inherited everything!'

'It was never like that. Charles made no secret of it. Craig's been out of the country the last six months, which is why he didn't come sooner.'

'He's going to live at Apperknowle?'

'For the time being. He's a writer.' It was stretching a point, but Rachel saw no reason to doubt his eventual success. With his mother gunning for him, he had it made. 'He's gone to London for a few days,' she added, 'but I'd like you to meet him when he gets back. If Keith's off duty at the weekend, why don't you come on over? Gemma too, of course. We can have a pool party if the weather's good enough.'

Lindsay looked a little uncertain. 'I'd have to look up his rota.'

She would know it off by heart, Rachel was sure, but she appreciated the reason for hesitation. 'Well, let me know,' she said easily. 'If not this next weekend, there'll be others.'

They went on from there to reminisce about former times, laughing at the memories of school escapades and girlish ambitions. By the time Rachel left, the two of them were more than halfway back to the friendship they had shared for so many years. Seated in the taxi she had ordered, she felt happier than in months. Lindsay and Keith had always been such a well-balanced couple, even as teenagers. Theirs was a marriage to emulate.

Hardly the kind she was likely to forge with Craig for a husband, came the thought, but she refused to allow it to depress her. The future was an unwritten book; who could tell what might happen?'

The week went by slowly and, for the most part, uneventfully. By Thursday evening, Rachel was beginning to wonder if Craig intended coming back at all. Perhaps, having had the opportunity to think the matter over, he had decided to back out of the agreement. The financial gain had been the only real incentive, and he obviously wasn't that short of money.

The telephone call just before ten o'clock elicited confusion on her part. He would be there Saturday afternoon, Craig said. As Lindsay had already phoned to say they couldn't manage this weekend, that presented no problem, but it still didn't explain why it was taking so long to sort out his affairs.

'Everything OK?' he asked into a pause. 'No problems cropped up that I should know about?'

'What others might there be?' she countered a little too tartly, and could sense the mocking smile.

'If I knew the answer I wouldn't be asking the question. Have you missed me?'

Her pulse quickened. 'Like a hole in the head,' she retorted crisply. 'How did you find your mother?'

'Unchanged,' he said.

'Not too upset because you came straight down here before looking her up?'

'She was out of the country herself until yesterday,' came the smooth response. 'We had a grand reunion last night.'

'Touching.' Rachel made no effort to soften the irony. 'And how did she react to...everything?'

'The way one might expect.' There was acerbity now in his own tone. 'She's looking forward to meeting you and judging for herself.'

Rachel went first hot and then cold. 'You didn't tell her all of it?'

'Every last detail, so she's one person you won't need to put up any pretence for.'

'You had no right!'

'I had every right. This is my life we're talking about too. What you choose to tell your mother is your affair. Only don't be too surprised if she guesses all isn't quite as it should be.'

Rachel swallowed on the hard lump in her throat. 'How did she take it?'

'The way she takes most things these days—philosophically. Not that the thought of being a grandmother exactly delights her as yet. She'll need to get used to the idea.'

'That's jumping the gun a bit,' Rachel protested. 'We're not even married yet.'

'Something else we have to thrash out when I get back.' He gave her no opportunity to reply to that statement. 'See you Saturday.'

Rachel put down the receiver with a hand that had developed a slight shake. Craig had sounded so relentless. Well, she could be that way too. Six months was surely not too long to wait?

She was out by the pool, basking under a sun turned unseasonably hot, when he put in an appearance. Opening her eyes to find him studying the lines of her body in the brief bikini with undisguised appreciation brought hot colour rushing to her cheeks.

'I—I didn't hear the car,' she stammered, sitting up to reach for her wrap.

'You wouldn't down here.' He was openly amused by her reaction. 'That's a nice tan you're developing. Be careful you don't overdo it.'

'I was just about to call it a day,' she lied. 'Did you have a good journey?'

'No better, no worse than before. It's a busy route.' He paused, expression giving no warning. 'I'd like you to meet my mother.'

Rachel's head turned as if on a pulley to the woman standing just outside her prior line of vision. The newcomer smiled and held out a hand.

'Hallo, Rachel. I'm Caroline.'

Tall, dark-haired and possessed of the kind of vibrantly alive good looks which made a mockery of time, the woman was nothing like the picture Rachel had built in her mind's eye. In the Chanel-styled suit of fine cream wool, and poised on three-inch heels, she looked more like a model than an editor. Her eyes were the same colour as her son's—and just as assessing.

'This is quite a surprise,' Rachel managed, taking the hand. 'Craig didn't tell me he would be bringing you with him.'

'A last-minute decision on my part, so don't take him too much to task. I'm due back for the monthly board meeting on Tuesday, so I shan't be in your hair too long.'

Rachel made a swift recovery. 'You're more than welcome. After all, Apperknowle is Craig's home too. It's only that I'd have liked time to have a room got ready for you.'

'It will be done while we're having tea,' Craig declared. 'I already saw Mrs Brantley about it. I ordered the trolley brought out here, by the way. We may as well take advantage of the weather.'

Caroline Lindhurst took the padded seat he drew up for her, leaving Rachel feeling at even more of a disadvantage on the lower lounger. Craig himself remained standing, hands thrust into the pockets of his fawn cord trousers as he scanned the pool surface.

'Looks ready for a clean,' he remarked.

'The contract company is due on Monday,' Rachel assured him, feeling ridiculously guilty of neglect. 'It was skimmed only this morning.'

'Just a comment,' he said. 'No cause for alarm. You keep the whole place in tip-top shape.'

'You mean the staff do.' She was unable to keep the tartness from her voice. 'I don't have to lift a finger.'

'But even staff have to be given orders,' he responded on a surprisingly mild note. 'That's an art in itself—especially if you're not born to it.'

'We were none of us that,' put in Caroline easily. 'I understand you were born on the island, Rachel?'

'That's right. My parents moved here soon after they were married.'

'No other relatives?'

'Just an aunt on my father's side in Manchester.' She made a gesture of dissent. 'Charles knew my background.'

'If it came across like an inquisition, I apologise.' The tone sounded sincere. 'I'm finding this situation rather difficult to handle—though no more, I'm sure, than you are yourself. Charles was entirely wrong to descend to emotional blackmail. No mere house can be worth what you're going through.'

'It isn't just a house,' Rachel protested, 'it's a whole bloodline. Even if I were to marry someone outside of the family who was willing to change his name by deed poll, it wouldn't be Lindhurst blood.'

'Charles really indoctrinated you, didn't he?' said Craig hardly. 'No sacrifice too great!'

'Not for me.' Rachel's jaw was set, blue eyes fired. 'Did you need your mother with you to tell me you're backing out?'

He took a step towards her, mouth suddenly grim, then stopped, glancing at the older woman with a faint, wry smile. 'You see what I'm up against?'

'You're wrong,' Caroline said. 'Craig has no intention of backing out. I'm here because I wanted to meet you. I'd say it's only natural that I would want to meet the girl my son is planning to marry, wouldn't you?'

Rachel felt the anger fade, leaving her flat and defenceless—though against what, she wasn't altogether sure. 'I suppose it is,' she got out. 'It must have come as quite a shock to you.'

'Fortunately I'm fairly resilient.' The older woman's tone was dry. 'I've had to be—especially these last few months while Craig's been missing——'

'What's past is best forgotten,' he cut in brusquely. 'Here's tea. Let's concentrate on that.'

Rachel bit back the question hovering on her lips. 'Missing' was very different in meaning from simple 'out of touch'. The fact that he wasn't prepared to talk about it signified some fairly traumatic experience. Whether she would ever have her curiosity satisfied was open to doubt on present showing.

Craig straddled one of the wrought-iron chairs, accepting the cup Rachel poured for him with a brief word of thanks. The thick dark hair had a healthy sheen in the sunlight. Cut to a crisp line at his nape, it merged with skin paler than the rest of his body, as if the hair had been worn quite a lot longer until fairly recently. It was the first time she had really noted it.

'I hardly expected to find myself sitting here like this at Apperknowle after Charles married again,' Caroline remarked. 'You knew you were his second wife, of course?'

'Naturally.' This time Rachel kept her tone strictly neutral. 'He could hardly have kept it a secret. The divorce was sixteen years ago.'

'Long before he received his peerage.' Caroline smiled. 'Debora might have played a better hand if she'd known what the future held.'

'You knew her?'

'Only by hearsay. Apparently she not only refused to give Charles a child, but was seeing other men on the side. The surprise is that he waited so long before marrying again, if a son and heir was his main interest.'

Not beyond shooting a barb or two, Rachel reflected wryly, meeting the grey eyes. So what should she expect? But for her, Craig might well have inherited the lot.

'I think he'd probably reconciled himself to it until he learned he was going to die,' she said expressionlessly. 'Then it was a case of finding someone young enough to offer a fair chance of success, and quickly enough to have the time.'

'And you didn't mind being...used that way?'

'I didn't see it that way.' The mask was slipping a little. 'Charles loved me just as I loved him. Nothing you or anyone else can say or do will ever change that.'

'If it's what you believe, I wouldn't even try,' came the smooth response.

'I think that's enough,' Craig interceded. 'The only thing of interest now is fulfilling the terms of the will.'

'Which will be when *I'm* good and ready, and not before,' Rachel flashed, releasing the anger and pain his mother had elicited.

His shrug belied the dangerous glint in his eyes. 'As you say, when you're good and ready. Now, supposing we change the subject? I thought we might all go out to dinner somewhere tonight. It would be a nice idea to get your mother to join us, if she's free.'

'I already ordered dinner here,' Rachel responded.

'And I already cancelled it. Where would you suggest we go?'

Her breath came out short and sharp. Half-owner or not, he was taking too much of a liberty. She would have liked to tell him exactly where he *should* go. She contented herself instead with a gesture implying indifference. 'You'll find restaurants listed in *Yellow Pages*. Make your own choice.'

'Now you're being childish,' he admonished.

'According to your initial summing up, that's all I am,' she shot back. 'Why expect anything else?' She got up, sliding her feet into the waiting sandals. 'I'll go and phone Mom now.'

Walking away, she could feel both pairs of eyes on her back. Caroline Lindhurst was not making any of this easier to bear. What she thought to achieve by coming here was difficult to guess. All she had done so far was drive the wedge even deeper.

As always on a Saturday afternoon, her mother was in the shop. She responded to the invitation with unanticipated enthusiasm.

'Nice of Craig to think of it,' she said. 'Where shall I meet you?'

'We didn't decide yet,' Rachel admitted. 'We'll pick you up instead. Around seven?'

She had made the call from the library. She was just replacing the receiver in its rest when Craig walked into the room.

'Assuming there's a copy of *Yellow Pages* in here, I'll make a start,' he said on a note mild enough to conjure sudden shame in her breast. He was right, she thought, it had been a childish gesture.

Eyes averted, she said, 'Farringford out the other side of Freshwater would be a good place. It was Tennyson's home.' She thumbed through the small table directory. 'That's the number.'

He made no immediate move to the telephone. Instead, he took hold of her arm just above the elbow, turning her towards him. Robbed of the extra height provided by high heels, Rachel found herself looking at the strong brown column of his throat beneath the open shirt collar, and had a sudden crazy desire to put her lips to the hollow.

'Shall we start again?' he asked softly.

Rachel still couldn't bring herself to meet the grey eyes. Only when he dropped his head to find her mouth with his did she come jerkily alive, pressuring back away from him with a terse, 'Don't!'

He held her fast, mouth a determined line. 'One thing we need to get clear. I'm not prepared to be repulsed every time I attempt to get closer. You need to let go of your girlish ideals and start acting like an adult. It's what Charles wanted, remember?'

'He didn't stipulate that I had to enjoy it,' she gritted. 'I don't have your ability to turn a blind eye to the circumstances.'

'You would have if you'd let yourself.' His grip had tautened. 'You might be repressed, but you're a long way from being frigid. Do you think I don't know what you're really feeling under all that "don't touch me" guff?'

'No, you don't know!' She was desperate to repudiate the idea. 'It's different for a man.'

'It certainly is.' There was irony in his voice. 'A woman can fake arousal. I'd have a definite problem if I didn't find you physically desirable.'

One hand came up to smooth her cheek lightly, the touch of his fingers sending a tremor the length of her spine. She froze as he slowly traced the curve of her jaw, wanting to move yet unable to summon the strength of will to resist any longer.

He used both hands to cup her face, lifting it to find her lips with his in a gentle brushing motion that set her

pulses hammering and sent a thrill like an electric shock
to every extremity. Somehow she found herself kissing
him back, her mouth softening, opening, inviting the
tingling, toe-curling caress of his tongue. Lost, said a
small voice at the back of her mind, but she paid it no
heed. Her whole being was concentrated on the exquisite
sensations.

The slow progress of one lean hand down the length
of her throat went unchecked by either movement or
desire. She drew in a sharp breath when he reached the
full, firm curve of her breast within the opened front of
her wrap, but still made no move to withdraw. Still
kissing her, he slid his fingers beneath the scanty strip
of material to explore the tender flesh with a touch that
was both pleasure and pain. Only not a pain she wanted
to stop, even when it made her gasp and writhe in his
arms.

The bikini-top was held in place by two sets of string
ties, one at her nape and the other at her centre back.
Craig had released both before she fully realised what
he was doing. Clad only in the triangular briefs and
flimsy wrap, she felt totally vulnerable. She attempted
to draw away, but he held her fast, tracing the line of
her spinal column with a sensitivity that tremored an
involuntary response.

'Don't be silly,' he said softly. 'It's the most natural
thing in the world both for me to want to touch you and
for you to want me too. You're a very sensual young
woman, if only you'd let yourself acknowledge it instead of fighting it. You felt the same way I did the
moment we set eyes on each other. Now admit it.'

'I hated you,' she denied thickly. 'I still do! Let me
go, Craig.'

His laugh was low. 'You don't mean that. If you hate anything, it's the fact that I can arouse something in you that Charles never did.'

Too close to the truth for comfort, Rachel conceded. Craig's kisses, the feel of his hands on her body, his whole masculine essence, overwhelmed every principle she held dear. Right now she was on the verge of giving way and answering the call he was making on her. Only that might well lead to something she wasn't ready for yet.

'It's already gone five,' she pointed out on a husky note. 'I told Mom we'd pick her up at seven, and you still have to make a reservation.'

There was a moment when it appeared he might not respond to the plea, then he gave a resigned sigh and let her go, bending to pick up the scrap of material from the floor where he had dropped it and hand it back to her. 'Till next time,' he said drily.

Clutching the silky folds of the wrap about her, Rachel moved away. From now on, she vowed shakily, she would take care to be fully dressed when Craig was around. Clothes were the only barrier she had left.

CHAPTER FIVE

SET within a fine park flooded with oak and pine trees, Farringford House was renowned for both food and atmosphere. Some of Lord Tennyson's books and items of furniture were still in residence.

'Where Emily Tennyson did her entertaining, I believe,' commented Caroline over coffee in the white Gothic décor of the drawing-room. 'Edward Lear, Arthur Sullivan—even the Prince Consort himself. If there's anything in this "stone tape" theory, these walls could probably tell a fine old tale!'

'Along with a lot of others,' agreed Laura. 'Apperknowle itself has quite a history. The passage running down to the beach from the cellars is said to have been used for smuggling in contraband brandy.'

The other woman looked interested. 'I didn't know that. My husband rarely discussed family history.'

'Maybe he didn't want it generally known that there were law-breakers in the family tree,' Craig put in smoothly. 'You didn't mention a secret passage, Rachel.'

'It was permanently blocked off years ago,' she advised. 'Though you can still see where the entrance was, if you know where to look. It came out at the back of a cave which was filled in by a cliff collapse.'

'Fascinating.' Caroline sounded genuinely intrigued. 'I'll have to delve further. Who knows what else the Lindhursts might have got up to in the past?'

Laura shook her head. 'Not all that much. Apart from one bad apple, they seem to have led fairly blameless lives all round. I've made something of a study since Rachel joined the clan.' She paused, tone altering a little. 'I thought there might be material for a book.'

Sculpted brows lifted. 'You write?'

'Only children's stories so far,' Laura replied on a wryly humorous note. 'Three rejection slips is all I've got to show for it, which is why I thought I might try another market.'

'Children's fiction is certainly one of the most difficult to break into,' Caroline conceded. 'All the same, you should persevere, if that's what you feel you're best at.' The hesitation was brief. 'We don't handle that line ourselves, but I could, perhaps, offer you an opinion. Only providing you have shoulders broad enough to take whatever I might find necessary to say, though.'

'You're in publishing?' Laura both looked and sounded covered in confusion. 'Oh, lord, what must you think of me? I mean, I knew Craig was planning on writing a book, but it didn't occur to me that you were in the business yourself. I only mentioned it at all because——' She broke off, and made a rueful gesture. 'I really didn't know. Rachel, why on earth didn't you say?'

Rachel looked her at parent bemusedly. 'It never occurred to me,' she admitted. 'How long have you been writing children's stories? You never mentioned it before.'

'About a year or so.' Laura was still obviously discomfited. 'Look, let's forget it, shall we?'

It was Craig who answered, a note of amusement in his voice. 'If you're serious about becoming a writer, you need to snatch any possible advantage available. An objective critique might prove invaluable.'

'It might also prove I'm absolutely no good,' she returned. She glanced in his mother's direction. 'In any case, I don't expect you to act on the offer.'

The other gave a smiling shrug. 'Faint heart never got one anywhere. You can give me what you have tonight, and I'll look them over. Why knows? We may have another Enid Blyton in the offing——'

'Considering what the critics have to say about her work these days, I shouldn't think that would prove such a wonderful thing,' cut in Rachel smartly, sensing condescension in the remark.

Caroline laughed. 'My dear, the general public takes little notice of that kind of pseudo-intellectual claptrap. I devoured Blyton in my time, and I dare say my grandchildren will do the same—if and when I acquire any, of course.'

Feeling the warmth invade her cheeks, Rachel ruefully acknowledged that she had asked for the dig. While Caroline was all for Craig's inheriting his share, she didn't have to like the conditions attached. It was unlikely that the two of them would ever develop a congenial relationship. They were more like sparring partners.

'That'll be the day,' said Craig lightly. 'Would anyone like another brandy or whatever?'

No one did, but the offer served its purpose in changing the subject. Rachel contributed little to the following twenty minutes or so of desultory conversation. Her mother's revelation had come as quite a shock. She had given no hint of her aspirations to become a writer. All she herself could hope now was that Caroline would let her down fairly lightly. After all, if three publishers had already rejected her work, it couldn't be all that good, could it?

They left at ten. Craig had insisted on driving the Mercedes, even if it did mean he couldn't have more than one glass of wine with dinner. If he had his way,

Grayson would be out of a job and the Rolls sold, Rachel suspected. While not particularly against losing the latter, she would fight to the death to retain the former. Where would Grayson find another job at his age?

Laura invited them all in for more coffee while she looked out the manuscripts Caroline had requested to see. Small as it was, the flat was both comfortable and decorative. The skilful arrangement of spring flowers and greenery occupying the hearth in lieu of a screen elicited admiring comment from Caroline.

'Something I could never do myself,' she admitted. 'I just tend to stick them in a vase and hope for the best.' She took the neat pile of folders Laura was proffering, and set them on her lap. 'Here's hoping you're as good with words as you are with flowers!'

There were plenty of other examples of her mother's artistic talents around, but pointing them out, Rachel reflected, might be gilding the lily just a little too much right now. She felt some sense of rebuff in not having been made privy to this other enthusiasm. Surely they were close enough still to have no secrets from one another?

But she had one herself, didn't she? came the instant and shaming reminder. And of far greater magnitude. Catching Craig's eye, she had the odd feeling that he knew exactly what was going through her mind. He had been totally honest with his mother; it was on the cards that he thought she should be the same with hers. Only that was beyond her—at present, anyway.

The drive back to Apperknowle was accomplished in near silence on Rachel's part. She had got into the rear seat without hesitation, leaving mother and son to share the front together. From where she sat, she kept seeing Craig's eyes as he glanced in the driving-mirror. Whether he could also see her, she wasn't sure. She kept her face carefully composed just in case, although the memory of that earlier episode in the library made it difficult. Muscle and sinew went into spasm at the very thought of being in his arms again. If he kept on making such attacks on her senses, she doubted her ability to hold out against him for the stated six months. Only to give in and allow him his way on the basis of pure weakness of spirit would be even more shameful. She had to keep on resisting him, no matter how hard the task.

Caroline announced her intention of going straight up to bed as soon as they got in. Taking a rare advantage of a reasonably early night, she said.

She had the manuscripts with her, Rachel noted as the older woman mounted the stairs. Whether for show or for genuine perusal remained open to question. She faked a yawn of her own for Craig's benefit.

'I think I'll follow suit. I'll leave it to you to decide how best to entertain your mother tomorrow.'

'Running away?' he asked softly as she made a move towards the staircase.

'Walking,' she corrected without turning her head. 'Goodnight.'

He caught her before she reached the bottom tread, swinging her about to pressure her lips apart in a kiss that left her shaken to the core.

'Sweet dreams,' he said with satire.

Rachel left him standing there, her legs like jelly as she went on up. If only he would leave her alone! she thought desperately. If only he would go away and not come back until it was absolutely essential!

And what good would that do? asked the small voice of reason. When the time came he would still be the same person—and so would she.

Surprisingly, she slept like a top, awakening at seven to bright sunlight and the sound of bird-song. The blackbird perched on the balcony rail eyed her with friendly expectancy when she stepped outside. Rachel crumbled one of the wheaten biscuits she always kept ready in her room, and fed the bird by hand as she had been doing since it was a fledgeling. It no longer came every morning now that other sources of food were readily available, but winter would no doubt renew the dependency again.

There was no sign of Craig down at the pool. Sparkling in the sunlight, the water was an invitation. The air itself felt warm enough on her skin, even at this hour, to tempt her into taking the plunge. Why not take advantage while the opportunity was there? Tomorrow they might well be back to grey skies and a cool north-easterly.

The deep blue one-piece suit she chose to don was cut high at the leg, but covered her in a way that made her feel infinitely more secure than the bikini she had worn the day before. That it also outlined her figure more distinctively was a detail she overlooked.

With her towelling bathrobe over the top, and sandals on her feet, she made her way down the rear stairs, calling a cheery greeting as she passed the open kitchen door. Mrs Brantley and Mrs Johnston, the cook, would be discussing household matters—among others—over a cup of tea, as they usually did at this time, while Doreen would be passing on the former's instructions to the two daily helps.

The house ran like clockwork; it left Rachel with little or nothing to do except plan menus for the week and check household accounts from time to time. She had never been bored in her life, she had told Craig, but it was a lie because she had been these past few weeks, since starting to recover from the utter despondency she had felt after losing Charles. Working with Craig on this book he was planning would be a godsend in more ways than one.

The water looked just as inviting in close-up. Sliding out of the towelling robe, she took a header into the pool, surfacing halfway down the length to smooth back her wet hair from her face. She should have fastened it up before she came in, but it was hardly worth the bother now.

She swam several lengths, employing first the crawl, then the breast-stroke, and finishing off with the butterfly before coming to a panting but exhilarated rest at the deep end.

'Nice style,' applauded Craig from the far side. 'A bit short on stamina, perhaps, after the winter lay-off, but practice will improve on that.'

He was wearing a pair of the briefest racing-trunks Rachel had ever seen; they certainly left little to the imagination. She could feel herself going first hot and then cold and then hot again, regardless of the constant temperature of the water in which she was immersed. A magnificent male animal, lithe as a panther and strong as a lion—and as dangerous to her peace of mind as both put together, came the thought.

'I suppose,' she said shortly, 'you're world class yourself?'

His laugh was light. 'If I were I'd be putting it to good use. I didn't expect to see you down here at this hour for at least another month, after what you said last week.'

'It wasn't as warm as this last week.' She was anxious to dispel any notion he might have that she was here in the hope of seeing him. 'In any case, the water is heated.'

'It was last week too.' The grey eyes surveyed her with unconcealed derision. 'If it isn't cold that's making you shiver, what could it be, I wonder?'

'I'm not shivering!' Her voice sounded too high-pitched; she made an effort to bring it down. 'Don't be ridiculous!'

'Trembling, then.' He was without mercy. 'You're looking anywhere but directly at me. Do I disturb you?'

'You disgust me!' she flung at him. 'Why bother putting anything on at all?'

'Why indeed?' He slid his fingers under the top band of his trunks as if to remove them, mouth slanting as Rachel made a hasty gesture of negation.

'I didn't mean that!'

'So watch the sarcasm,' he reproved. 'I don't find skinny-dipping in the least embarrassing myself.'

Rachel stayed where she was as he dived into the pool. Her arms were aching where they stretched along the side-rail, but she couldn't bring herself to leave hold. Craig had known she was down here; he had worn the skimpy trunks deliberately to taunt her. There was a painful knot in her stomach—a feeling almost as if she had been kicked. She fought to wipe all expression from her eyes as he surfaced in front of her.

'You could take that off and sample freedom for yourself,' he said without mockery. 'There has to come a time when we'll be together minus the trappings, so why not make a start now?'

'The circumstances are hardly the same,' she forced out between teeth that wanted to clench and stay clenched. '*I'm* not into skinny-dipping!'

'The circumstances are what we make of them,' he said. 'Right now I have a powerful need to make love to you.' He came up close, putting both hands to the rail either side of her so that she was trapped. 'Like this.'

She twisted her head away in an attempt to escape the seeking mouth, but it was a futile exercise. He brought his whole body into contact with hers as he kissed her, drawing a smothered moan to her lips as she felt the demanding hardness of him. He was already aroused and making no bones about it, moving against her in a manner that sent tremor after tremor coursing through her.

Instinct took over to open her thighs and fit her to him in the age-old unity, her mind already resenting the barriers still between them. She kissed him back feverishly, wantonly, wrapping her arms about his neck in a sudden uncontrollable frenzy of desire such as she had never known before.

It took the disappearance of the sun behind a passing cloud to bring her out of it. Robbed of that sparkling light, the pool surface looked cold and grey and utterly devoid of comfort. She thrust him away with a strength that took them both by surprise, diving for the safety of the step-ladder a few feet away, and hauling herself from the water. She was shivering for real now, and unable to stop. How could she ever face him again after this?

Craig made no attempt to follow her as she snatched up her robe and headed for the house. When she did glance back, on reaching the terrace, he was still in the water, moving in a fast and powerful crawl that took him end to end in seconds. That the pace was the product of anger, she didn't need telling. She had left him frustrated after leading him on to believe she was ready to go the whole way. Intentional or not, it had been a despicable way to behave.

Showered and dressed in peach cotton trousers and shirt, she put off going down to breakfast as long as she possibly could. The temptation to stay up here in her room was strong, but the knowledge that she was going to have to get it over with some time made the gesture pointless. What she needed was to affect the kind of blasé attitude other women with whom Craig was acquainted would no doubt bring to the occasion.

Both he and Caroline were already at the table when she finally went down. The latter looked cool and casual in a skirt and matching top of cream knitted cotton.

'Craig thought you might have gone back to bed after your exertions,' she commented. 'Enjoy your morning swim, did you?'

Blue eyes met unreadable grey, and slid away again. There was no way, Rachel was sure, that he would have told his mother everything. It would hardly show him in a very good light.

'Up to a point,' she returned with commendable nonchalance, taking her seat. 'Have you thought about what you'd like to do today?'

'Are you asking me, or Craig?' came the somewhat pointed query.

'Well...you, I suppose.' Rachel could feel herself already beginning to flounder. She made a supreme effort to regain lost ground, looking directly at the man seated opposite. 'Unless you have any good ideas?'

The twitch of a muscle in his jawline was the only indication that her barb had registered. His tone was certainly level enough. 'I might have one or two. How about taking a run over to Carisbrooke? I've yet to see the castle myself. We could have a pub lunch somewhere afterwards.'

'Better than sitting around twiddling our thumbs,' agreed Caroline smoothly. 'I'd like to have a word with your mother some time today. Perhaps this afternoon, if she isn't tied up.'

'I could find out,' Rachel acknowledged with reticence. She added hesitantly, 'I hope you won't be too hard on her.'

Caroline lifted an eyebrow. 'You don't seem to have much faith in her abilities.'

'Of course I do!' There was more than a touch of self-recrimination in the denial. 'She's always been very creative. A lot of the things she sells she makes herself. In season she does a roaring trade at the shop.'

'And spends the winter just ticking over, I suppose?' The shrug was expressive. 'Not wholly fulfilling for a woman on her own, which is why I imagine she turned to writing as an outlet.' Her eyes went to her son, who was listening expressionlessly. 'An excellent escape, wouldn't you say?'

His reply was brief. 'It can be.'

Rachel looked from one to the other in some confusion. 'Are you saying you like Mom's stories?'

'That,' said Caroline, 'is something I'm only prepared to discuss with Laura herself. In fact, it might be a good idea if the two of us got together on our own. If you'll give me her phone number, I'll contact her myself and make the arrangement. You won't mind if I leave you two to your own devices after lunch?'

It was Craig who answered. 'I'm sure we can find plenty to do. Right, Rachel?'

This time she couldn't bring herself to look at him. 'Right,' she murmured.

She was heartily relieved when the meal was over and she could leave the table without appearing to be running away again. However she spent this afternoon, she would not be spending it alone with Craig; that much she could say with certainty. So far as the future went, that was something she had to come to terms with. Just not yet. She wasn't ready. If he would only give her time!

Despite everything, the trip to Carisbrooke turned out to be enjoyable. It was several years since Rachel had visited the castle, and she had forgotten how atmospheric the place was.

Although so early still in the season, the tourists were quite thick on the ground. Caroline was disinclined to stand in the queue to watch the donkey treadmill, preferring instead to climb the ramparts of the Norman keep for an overall view of the fort and town.

'Well worth the visit,' she declared on leaving. 'In fact, the island itself could prove a nice place to retire to when the time comes.'

'Which won't be until you're tossed out by force, if I know you,' observed Craig drily. 'You'd go crazy just sitting around.'

Caroline laughed. 'I didn't mean retirement from life! I hope and trust that my mind will still be active even after my body slows down. I might even take up writing myself. Memoirs have a ready market, providing they're lively enough. Mine would certainly be that.'

Craig grinned. 'You can say that again!'

Listening to the exchange, Rachel felt a complete outsider. Mother and son were obviously close, though without being cloying about it. Even as Craig's wife in time to come, she would still be no closer to the kind of relationship necessary for a marriage to last. It was Craig himself who had pointed out the lack of compulsion to stay together once the actual condition had been met, although whether he would still feel the same way if and when they had a child was anyone's guess.

There was no point in thinking about that now, she resolved. Getting through the coming months was concern enough.

They drove over to Brading for lunch in an 'olde worlde' public house which offered a surprisingly varied and interesting menu.

'Pity we shan't have time to do the museum,' remarked Craig over coffee. 'It looks as if it could be fun.'

'There's no reason why you and Rachel shouldn't come back during the week, is there?' asked his mother. 'You're not planning on starting work on the book right away, I should hope. You need a little R and R after what you've been through.'

Rest and recuperation was what she meant, Rachel assumed. Caroline herself was obviously under the impression that what Craig *had* been through was no secret. How little she knew.

'What I need,' he said levelly, 'is something to occupy my mind. Hands too,' he added on a note that brought Rachel's chin up. 'I'm more than ready to go.'

'Creative fever?' Rachel heard herself saying with an irony that was simply asking for trouble.

The spark which briefly lit the grey eyes was a danger signal in itself. 'Something like that. Are you still willing to help out?'

'With the re-typing? Of course.' Rachel found time to wonder where her cool composure was coming from. The day was a long way from being over. 'I can always close my eyes if it all becomes too much for me to handle.'

Just for a moment his lips seemed to twitch. 'It's one way, I suppose. I'll hope not to offend your sensibilities too much.'

'Always remembering that it's the hot spots the public goes for,' put in Caroline drily. 'Soft pedalling rarely makes a bestseller. Write it as it comes. God knows, you've got the experience!'

This time the amusement was open. 'Some. What time did you arrange to see Laura?'

'Around two-thirty.' Caroline glanced at her watch. 'It's a quarter-past now, so we'd better be going. You can pick me up again at four. That will give the two of you time to sort out whatever it is that's causing the sniping between you.'

It was going to take more than an hour or so, thought Rachel wryly, avoiding Craig's eyes as they got to their feet. A whole lot more!

They didn't call in at the flat. Leaving his mother on the pavement outside the shop, Craig drove straight off. He hadn't asked Rachel where she would like to spend the next hour and a half, nor would she have known what to tell him if he had. One place was as good as another, she supposed, to have the confrontation she could sense was coming. So much for spending the afternoon alone.

He drove along the coast road towards the looming white heights of Culver Cliffs. There were plenty of people on the beach, and a fair number in the sea. The hardy British holiday-maker, Rachel reflected. No matter how cold the water, bathing was a must. The strange thing was that since leaving school there had been summers when she had hardly set foot on the beach herself—which was true of many residents. One tended to take it for granted simply because it was there, within easy reach all the time.

Craig turned into a hotel car park just before the road curved inland, bringing the car to a stop, facing the sea.

'Too late to offer you a drink,' he said, 'but a good place to talk.'

Rachel steeled herself for what was sure to be a pretty distasteful conversation, to be totally taken aback by his first words.

'I owe you an apology,' he began. 'Things got a little out of hand this morning. Patience, I'm afraid, was never one of my virtues.'

Rachel found her voice with difficulty, hardly knowing what to say in return. 'I think I got a bit carried away myself.'

'Not to the point of losing control,' he replied on a dry note. 'Another couple of minutes and I'd have been past the point of no return. Considering where we were at the time, that could have proved embarrassing for us both.'

'Is that the only reservation you have?' she shot at him in a swift resumption of hostility.

'No, it isn't, so cool down,' he admonished. 'I was premature.' His lips slanted briefly. 'In a manner of speaking. I didn't come down to the pool with the intention of making you there and then, believe it or not.'

'But you did intend making me realise what I might be missing,' she retorted in a sardonic tone that widened his mouth into a slow smile.

'And I guess it worked at that.'

Her throat went suddenly dry. She swallowed hard, then said thickly, 'I'm sure you're well accustomed to driving women crazy with desire for your body. Why should I be an exception? The difference being that I don't happen to think it's enough on its own.'

'Without love, you mean?' He paused, expression unrevealing. 'It could develop.'

'Not in a million years!' The denial was forceful. 'You're not my type, Craig. Any more than I'm yours!'

'Too young for you?' The mockery was back full force. 'I'm getting older by the minute. Anyway, there's no altering things. Not unless you've changed your mind about carrying out Charles's wishes, that is?' He waited a moment, registering with growing cynicism the struggle openly displayed in her face. 'Integrity versus morality—a difficult choice. Supposing I give you a little help?'

She put both hands flat against his chest as he reached for her, desperate to keep him away from her. 'Don't! I don't want you touching me, Craig!'

'You've said that before,' he rejoined. 'And with just as little conviction. You might not like me all that much, but there are certain functions you can't control.' One hand covered the swell of her breast, fingers seeking and finding the tingling, peaking hardness of her nipple through the thin material of her blouse. 'Like this, for instance.'

His touch inflamed her; she suddenly wanted to seize the hand and press it to her until it hurt, to feel his lips bruising hers, to have control stripped from her with a ruthlessness that would brook no denial. It was only the memory of where they were that kept her from giving way to that urge.

'Leave me alone,' she gasped, and was mortified to hear the note of pleading in her voice. 'Just leave me alone!'

He continued to caress her for several more tumultuous seconds, looking into her eyes with a heart-stopping glitter in his own. Then the flame was damped down, the hand removed and a mask donned.

'I'll leave you alone,' he said. 'For now.'

Rachel sat motionless and silent as he switched on the engine and put the car into tyre-screeching reverse, only then conscious of the seatbelt still bisecting her breasts. The aching was nothing to do with the pressure, she knew; it went deeper than that. If only, she thought hollowly, she could view the situation the same way Craig obviously viewed it. Love didn't mean a thing to him.

CHAPTER SIX

LAURA answered the doorbell herself. She looked, Rachel thought, as if a lamp had been lit inside her.

'Come on up,' she invited. 'Caroline isn't in any hurry to get back, if you're not?'

'Nothing to rush back for,' Craig assured her with an irony Rachel hoped she was the only one to detect. 'I gather the news is good?'

'The best!' The eyes Rachel had inherited sparkled afresh. 'Your mother thinks I'm publishable as I stand. I can still hardly believe it!' Just for a moment a certain hesitancy took over. 'She wouldn't just say it because of the circumstances, would she?'

Craig's laugh was all the reassurance needed. 'Not unless she's totally altered character. Where work is concerned, she's as ruthless as she has to be. Believe me, if she thought you didn't have what it takes, she wouldn't have wrapped it up.'

Like mother, like son, reflected Rachel. She made an effort to shrug off despondency for her mother's sake. The latter merited her full attention and admiration.

'It's absolutely wonderful!' she exclaimed with slightly overdone enthusiasm. 'A writer in the family! It must have been fate that brought Caroline here this weekend.'

They had reached the top of the stairs leading up to the flat. Craig urged the two of them ahead into the living-room. Rachel could feel him close at her back, although he didn't touch her in any way. She was sensitised to his body heat, she realised. Hardly surprising.

Her breast still retained the imprint of those lean fingers after more than an hour of somewhat aimless driving around.

Caroline occupied one of the two comfy armchairs with an air of relaxation. 'Hi, kiddies,' she greeted them. 'Built any nice sand-castles?'

'None worth boasting about,' returned her son equably. 'Been playing Lady Bountiful, I hear.'

'With good cause.' Her smile was directed at Laura. 'I wasn't all that far out when I mentioned Blyton. Modernised version, of course. Today's pre-teens are far more likely to relate to a magic computer than a wishing-tree. Anyway, I know just the firm to approach.' The smile took on a slant reminiscent of her son's. 'I'm fairly well acquainted with the editorial director.'

'Would they be as likely to take Mom's stuff if she submitted it the normal way?' asked Rachel, regretting the comment immediately as she saw her mother's expression alter. 'Sorry,' she proffered. 'I didn't mean that the way it sounded.'

'What you did mean is does who you know make the difference between acceptance and rejection?' Caroline sounded quite calm about it. 'If you had any idea at all of the financial risks involved in launching a new author, you wouldn't need to ask that question. There's no editor alive going to take that risk without a fair certainty of success, no matter who does the asking.'

'But I have had those three rejections,' Laura reminded her, losing some of her glow. 'Whoever sent those obviously didn't think very highly of my work.'

'Probably because you submitted to the wrong people—or perhaps because the copy readers simply didn't recognise the potential. Unsolicited material normally goes through to an editor for further evaluation only if it's thought to hold promise. Otherwise we'd be snowed under.'

'So, in effect, having someone like you on my side does make a difference?' Laura asked.

Caroline shrugged. 'Well, yes, in that sense. I'll be making sure your manuscripts are seen by someone able to make a true assessment. Nothing wrong in that, is there?'

'No, I'm not against it.' Laura had regained her former ebullience. 'I'm only too grateful for the interest you're taking. You could easily have pretended to read through my stories and told me they were no good.'

The other lifted a delicate eyebrow in assumed indignation. 'Now would I do a thing like that?'

'It's not unknown,' put in Craig drily. 'Anyway, congratulations, Laura. I'd say you were well on your way to making your fortune.'

'Your turn next,' she replied, then paused in sudden embarrassment. 'Not that you're not already established as a writer, of course.'

'Journalist,' he corrected. 'Not quite the same thing as writing a novel. I've yet to prove myself there.'

'But you will, of course,' said Rachel, unable to resist the opportunity to take a dig at him. 'The word "failure" isn't in your vocabulary!'

'I try not to let it be,' he agreed without revealing any reaction apart from a slight narrowing of his lips. 'With a little help from the right quarters, I expect to do very well.'

Laura looked from one to the other with a faintly puzzled expression, as if not quite certain whether or not the acrimony was imaginary on her part. Rachel sensed her deciding that it must be, and underlined that decision with a bright smile.

'You're a real dark horse, Mom!'

'We all have our secrets,' said Craig blandly. 'I dare say there are things you've kept to yourself at times.'

'Such as not telling me you were marrying Charles until it was too late to stop it,' Laura agreed with an irony of her own. 'Not that I could have, of course. You were of age.'

Caroline said softly, 'I gather you didn't care for my brother-in-law very much?'

'As a husband for my daughter, no. He took an unfair advantage.'

'He did not!' Rachel was sitting on the extreme edge of her seat, fists clenched, face hot. 'You none of you knew him the way I did!'

'Obviously.' Craig looked unmoved by the force of her denial. 'It's all in the past, in any case. I think we should agree to leave it there.'

'Yes, you're right,' said Laura apologetically. 'I'm sorry, Rachel; I shouldn't have brought Charles into it.'

'It's all right.' Still trembling with anger and hurt, Rachel subsided back into her seat. 'I'm sorry too. There's nothing must spoil today for you. It's a red-letter one.'

The three of them stayed until five. Caroline and her mother seemed to have hit it off on a personal level too, Rachel noted dully. She felt like the odd one out again—even more so considering that this was her home ground, so to speak. If the assessment of worth turned out to be correct, a whole new career path would open up for her parent—perhaps even including a move away from the island. Certainly there would be no point in taking the tea-room plans any further. She didn't begrudge that opportunity, but it would leave her with no one to turn to.

She was getting way ahead of herself, came the soothing thought. If it happened at all, it wasn't likely to be next week.

For once Apperknowle failed to effect its usual welcome. Even after Charles had died, it had still been home; at the moment it was just a house Rachel happened to share. As a Lindhurst by birth, Craig held the greater right to it all. She was here simply to provide the propagation unit. No matter how convinced she was of Charles's regard for her, that was what it all came down to in the end.

'I'm going up to change,' announced Caroline when they were inside. 'I assume we'll be having dinner here tonight?'

'That's right,' Craig confirmed. 'A nice quiet family affair.'

'We're not a family!' Rachel jerked out, and felt her arm taken in grip of steel as he pulled her round to face him.

'But we will be,' he stated grimly. 'Make no mistake about that!'

'It's still my ultimate choice,' she reminded him, refusing to be intimidated by his anger. 'I can still back out of the arrangement.'

'And leave here?' He shook his head. 'You'll not do that. You know it, and I know it.'

'Don't count on it!' She was too incensed to care what she said. 'I'm beginning to realise that Charles might have asked just a little too much!'

They had both forgotten Caroline, who had halted with one foot on the bottom tread of the staircase. 'If you'll take my advice,' she said levelly, 'you'll go somewhere a little more private to thrash things out. Unless you want the staff to know all your business, that is.'

Craig was the first to make a move. 'You're quite right. The library, I think.'

'No!' Rachel jerked herself free of him with a strength she hadn't known she possessed. 'There's nothing more to say!'

Caroline made no attempt to stop her as she passed. She took the stairs at a rate that tautened a band across her chest by the time she reached the top. Craig hadn't followed her, which was something to be thankful for. At the moment she felt incapable of facing any more.

The following couple of hours seemed like a lifetime. Rachel spent most of it laid out on one of the balcony loungers, until the cooler evening air began to penetrate. She felt a little better after a shower and a change of clothing. The bright red dress she donned was by way of a statement. With lipstick to match, and heavier eye make-up than she was accustomed to wearing, she looked reassuringly poised and in command of herself. What she had to do now was act that way too, regardless of what she was feeling inside.

Caroline was in the drawing-room with a gin and tonic already to hand. 'I helped myself,' she said lightly. 'I was sure you wouldn't object.'

Rachel gave an equally light shrug. 'Feel free. You've more right here than I have.'

'It's a bit late to start feeling bitter about it all,' came the cool response. 'You should have told Charles "no" when he first brought the subject up. You might not have stood to inherit as much, but at least your conscience would have been clear.' She paused. 'That is what's bothering you, I take it?'

Rachel bit her lip. 'I suppose you think that's pretty stupid of me?'

'Not so much stupid as self-centred. You stand to inherit a substantial income whatever happens; Craig finishes up with nothing if you refuse to go through with the marriage. Not that I agree with the way Charles handled things, but that's not the question.' Her voice hardened a fraction. 'I don't intend standing by and seeing you rob my son of his rightful dues, Rachel. He doesn't deserve it.'

'I'll fight my own battles,' said Craig grimly from the doorway, where he had appeared unobserved by either party. 'Stay out of it, please, Mother.'

'Someone has to say it,' she retorted, undaunted by his tone. 'You don't need this, Craig. Not on top of these last few months.'

Rachel spat the words through clenched teeth. 'I am sick and tired of hearing about all you've been through these last few months!'

'You haven't,' Craig returned baldly. 'Nor will you be doing.'

'Why?' she demanded. 'Was it something you're ashamed of?'

She wanted to withdraw the taunt the moment she had made it, but it was too late. The lean features looked suddenly almost gaunt in their jaw-clamped tension.

'In a way, you might be right,' he said.

'Don't be ridiculous!' Caroline both sounded and looked disgusted. 'It was hardly your choice!'

'Forget it,' he returned briefly. He moved towards the drinks cabinet, glancing expressionlessly in Rachel's direction to ask, 'What will you have?'

Subdued by the knowledge that she had gone too far, she took the lead he was offering. 'Sherry, please.'

There was an uncomfortable silence in the room while he poured the drinks. Seated on one of the brocade sofas,

Rachel accepted the slender-stemmed glass from him when he brought it over, without lifting her gaze further than the cuff of his brown shirt. He was wearing pale cream trousers which fitted his hip-line the way good tailoring should, and which brought dryness to her throat. His wrist was supple, the tiny hairs on it bleached almost golden in comparison with those on his head. Wherever he had spent these past few months, he hadn't been deprived of sun.

He took a seat on the sofa opposite at his mother's side. 'You'll be better taking the Portsmouth crossing from Ryde and getting straight on the train tomorrow,' he said. 'What time were you thinking of leaving?'

'Any time after lunch will do,' Caroline answered. 'I'm not planning on doing very much with the evening, apart from sorting out a few bits and pieces. When do you get the Jag back, by the way?'

'Your guess is as good as mine,' Craig acknowledged. 'I'll have to give them a ring.'

'Well, don't let them mess around. John Murray was kept waiting over six weeks while they located spares.'

Rachel kept her eyes on her glass as they talked, not at all sure how she was going to get through the rest of the evening if they continued to shut her out. She might deserve it in part, but it wasn't going to help anything.

Caroline resolved the problem for her a moment or two later. There was no trace of animosity in her expression as she glanced across. 'If things work out the way I'm sure they will, your mother will be taking a trip up to town herself shortly. I've suggested she stay at my place. Hotels can be very lonely places.'

'You really are confident, aren't you?' Rachel answered, and saw the other woman's eyebrows lift.

'Yes, I am. Do you have still have doubts?'

'No,' Rachel replied hastily. 'I'm sure you know your job backwards.'

Caroline laughed. 'I wouldn't say I never make mistakes, but there's never been a total disaster as yet. Anyway, we'll see what we'll see.' She sobered again to add, 'The main thing is to get you two sorted out.'

'I told you to leave it,' growled Craig, fazing her not a bit.

'That would be neglecting my parental duty, darling. However...' she gave a resigned sigh '...I'll say no more for now, if that's what you really want.'

She kept her word for the rest of the evening. Laughing, joking, generally effervescent, she even managed to lighten the atmosphere. Rachel found herself unable to maintain her antipathy at its peak; whatever her views, Caroline Lindhurst was a character impossible wholly to dislike. Had the circumstances been different, they might even have become friends in time.

Craig appeared to have put the whole matter out of mind. Only on the odd occasion when she caught his eye did Rachel suspect that the composure was surface only. Tomorrow, after his mother had gone, he would be reopening the question; there was nothing surer than that. What her response would be, she still couldn't decide with any certainty. It was going to be a night of soul-searching.

Around eleven, it was Caroline who made the first move towards retiring. Tomorrow was likely to be an extended day, she said, so another early night wouldn't hurt. Rachel followed suit, leaving Craig to his own devices. The latter seemed in no hurry. They left him stretched in a chair with a glass to hand and an air of being there for the duration.

The two of them went upstairs in silence. Only when they reached the gallery, where they were to go separate ways, did Caroline pause to make a typically frank comment.

'You're going to have to make up your mind, you know. Matters can't be allowed to go on like this.'

'We still have six months, minus a week or so,' Rachel replied tonelessly. 'The marriage would still be valid even if we contracted it with hours to spare.'

'And you intend making Craig wait till the last possible moment to know his fate, is that it?' Caroline shook her head. 'What did he do to make you so vindictive towards him?'

'I scarcely know him,' Rachel burst out. 'Would you be so eager to marry a man you didn't know?'

'On a practical note, it would depend on what I stood to gain.'

'I'm not talking practicalities, I'm talking emotions.' Rachel's voice shook. 'I don't even like him!'

'But you are attracted to him,' came the unmoved response. 'The same way he is to you. The air fairly sizzles when the two of you look at each other.'

'That's simple animosity,' Rachel denied, and saw the older woman's mouth take on a slant.

'All part and parcel. A little healthy spleen keeps a relationship out of the doldrums. You'll not do better than my son. He's a real man, not one of those new breed of wimps! Handle him the right way, and you could still rule the roost.'

'I don't want to rule the roost.' Rachel was already turning away. 'Goodnight.'

'If the truth were known, I don't think you know *what* you want,' came the acerbic response. 'Pleasant dreams, anyway.'

The cut-off had been less than polite, Rachel knew, but Caroline had no business interfering. She was naturally biased where her son was concerned. That opinion wasn't going to influence Rachel in any way. She couldn't allow it to do so. Craig was only in this for the money; she was the one who stood to lose the most.

The night was fine, with just a bit of a spring chill in the breeze. She left the balcony door open to allow fresh air to circulate. Moonlight cast waving shadows on the figured plaster ceiling, making some of the relief work appear to move. So often she had lain here watching those same shadows while Charles had slept fitfully at her side.

His face was becoming difficult to conjure in her mind's eye, repeatedly being overruled by another set of younger, harder features with steely grey eyes and a mocking mouth. She stirred restlessly, recalling every detail of the lean body—the feel of him against her. It wasn't so much the act itself that she missed so badly, but the emotional contact. She needed to be loved, to love back—to lose herself in the process of proving that love. Charles had been a wonderful lover: gentle, considerate, wholly concerned with her pleasure and comfort. Craig——

Rachel cut off her thoughts right there, turning on her side to bury her face in the pillows and pray for sleep. No good could come of imagining. No good at all.

The caressing touch of the hand at her breast brought her back to slow dawning consciousness. Not like Charles to waken her in the night, she thought dreamily, but the response he was eliciting in her was no dream. She could feel the warmth of him at her back, not too close, but near enough to sense that he was already aroused. She pressed back instinctively towards him, heard him draw in a harsh breath.

Still only partially awake, she felt his hand leave her breast to slide the full length of her body and find the hem of her nightdress. Fingers traced a feather-light pattern over her lower leg, lingering to caress the tender skin at the back of her knee in a manner that made every nerve in her jump. He had never done that before—never conjured quite such wonderful sensation. She wanted more of the same, wanted more of everything. Dear, darling Charles!

The hand moved on, causing her to tremble in half-fearful anticipation as he smoothed the inner skin of her thighs. Some primitive sense of self-preservation clenched her muscles tight against that intrusion for a moment, but only for a moment because he wasn't about to be denied. A moan broke from her lips at the exquisite feeling, and her whole body went rigid before beginning to move involuntarily to the tune of his possession. There had never been a time when she had felt like this—as if all the world were tilting and spinning. There was a roaring sound in her ears, a gathering tumult inside her. The eruption, when it came, was overwhelming, like nothing she had ever experienced before. She felt totally drained yet wholly stimulated at one and the same time.

'Charles,' she murmured dazedly, turning towards him. 'Oh, Charles!'

The warm, hard, naked body tensed. Rachel suddenly came alive to reality as hands and other senses recognised the differences. Not Charles, but Craig. How could she not have known?

He threw an arm across her as she made a jerky move to leap from the bed, pressing her back into the pillows as he raised himself on an elbow above her.

'Too late for retreat,' he said gruffly. 'We'll take it from here.'

'No!' Rachel put up an arm against his chest and pushed with all her strength and desperation. 'Get away from me! I don't want you!'

'You just gave lie to that statement,' he said. 'You're ready for me right this minute. Vibrating with it, in fact!'

'I thought it was Charles,' she claimed fervently, and saw the strong mouth briefly widen.

'You might tell yourself that, but your body knew the difference. I could feel the surprise in you—the discovery. If you shut it out at all it was because you wanted it to continue. Because you couldn't stop yourself responding. And having come this far, we're not going back. I don't care if it takes all night to make you admit it; you're going to in the end!'

Rachel let the ineffective arm drop back. No amount of physical power she was capable of exerting was going to deter him from his purpose; that was more than obvious. All she had left was emotional appeal.

'I can't be like you and just live for the moment,' she whispered. 'I can't, Craig!'

'Yes, you can.' He put his lips to the hollow of her throat, using the very tip of his tongue to set the pulse there fluttering like a trapped bird. 'You can be whatever you want to be. Forget the other issues and just concentrate on enjoying what we have—the way I'm going to do.'

With no other recourse open to her, Rachel sought refuge in a bid to freeze him out. Only it wasn't going to be easy to control her body's responses, she realised at once as he moved his lips in a series of tiny kisses down to the tender swell of her breasts.

Her nightdress was held by narrow straps over the shoulders. Craig slid both of them down her arms, managing both to bare her to the waist and pinion her at one and the same time. The touch of his tongue was agony of a kind she couldn't bear—to stop. He traced the aureola in slowly diminishing circles until he finally reached her peaking nipple, taking it between his teeth in a combination of nibbling and sucking that drove her wild.

She was hazily aware of his hands pushing the clinging material further down her body, and found her arms released again as the straps slid away. Her fingers came up without volition to bury themselves in the thick dark hair, while her back arched to bring her into even greater prominence for the marauding mouth. Any notion she might have entertained of remaining cold to his caresses was driven from her by the overwhelming force of mounting desire. She wanted this man more than she had ever wanted anything in her life before—with an intensity that was close to feral. Nothing else mattered at the moment but that.

This time it was his own name that broke from her lips in an agonised whisper. She took her hands from his hair to run them down over broad shoulders, thrilling to the smooth ripple of muscle beneath warm, bare skin. His back tapered to narrow waist and hip, the latter hard and flat at the sides, lifting to firm twin hemispheres over which she lingered in newly awakened delight. She had never explored Charles like this—had never even thought of it. With Craig she needed to know every detail.

His breathing roughened as she drifted a hand back across his hipbone to find him. The movement came naturally to her, drawing a groan from him as his teeth clenched. He stood it for only a moment or two before calling a halt, pinning her to the mattress with the full weight of his body as he came over her.

'Not yet,' he said softly. 'Not until neither of us can hold out a moment longer!'

For her that moment wasn't going to be long in coming, Rachel thought dementedly as he began a pilgrimage down the full length of her body. She was already on fire both inside and out. Muscle and sinew quivered beneath the caressing movement of tongue and lip, just for a second or two stiffening and resisting the ultimate invasion. But only for a second or two, because she wanted this too, the way she wanted everything and anything he could do to her. She thrust a hand into her mouth to choke off the scream torn from the depths of her being.

Her limbs were pliable when he at last lifted himself back into position. She met him halfway, desperate for the feel of him inside her, for the strength and driving purpose of the hard male loins. They slid together with ease, with familiarity, with gratification, moved together in total harmony until the moment of release could be restrained no longer by either. Rachel was incapable of stifling her cry as she felt the pulsing life flooding her. Too late now, came the fleeting thought before everything merged into one great twirling wheel and lights went off in her head.

Awareness returned gradually—first of the weight of Craig's body trapping her beneath him, then of the heat he still generated. His head was on her shoulder, his breath warm on her neck, the whole lean length of him fitted to her as if it belonged nowhere else. She could feel his ribcage, the bands of muscle across his midriff and abdomen, the pressure of his thighs. They were still joined as one, she realised.

'Don't move,' he murmured, feeling her stir. 'Not just yet. I want to stay here holding you like this.'

Rachel subsided again, but only in the physical sense. Her mind was a turmoil of conflicting emotions. What had happened between them just now made any kind of withdrawal difficult. If nothing else, there was the question of possible results to be taken into account. Pregnancy might have been the ultimate aim of the union, but never so soon. How could she ever face anyone again if tonight's efforts should prove positive?

'Let me go, Craig,' she forced out huskily. 'Please!'

He lifted his head to look at her, his expression too shadowed to be read with any accuracy. 'Where's the point in fighting it any longer?' he asked on a low, rough note. 'We both of us knew it had to happen. Give me a few minutes more and it's going to happen again. That's the effect you have on me.' He paused, eyes dropping to her quivering mouth. 'The effect we have on each other. Can you honestly tell me you don't want me again?'

'I—don't—want—you.' Every word was an effort.

'You're not even a very accomplished verbal liar,' he scoffed without malice. He made an experimental movement, smiling at her automatic and uncontrollable reflex. 'You see? More than ready. I always did envy the female recovery rate.' He dropped his head again to find her mouth, murmuring against her lips, 'Not that it's going to take long for me either, you little witch. I can't have enough of you!'

It was as much the way he said it as the actual content that roused her to forget about protesting for the moment. She started kissing him back hungrily, almost savagely, wrapping her legs about him as she felt the wonderful mounting pressure of his renewal. There was going to come a time when she would hate herself for giving way with such utter abandonment, a fading voice warned, but that was later and this was now, and she could hold out no longer.

They must have fallen asleep afterwards, because when Rachel opened her eyes again it was getting light. Craig had rolled on to his side, although he still had an arm across her waist. His mouth in repose lost none of its firmness; she had to smother an urge to reach out and touch her fingers to the lips that had given her such infinite pleasure in the night.

How she was going to cope from here on in, she couldn't begin to think. It was going to take every ounce of control she could summon even to look him in the eye again without giving herself away entirely. She had fought so hard against allowing herself to love him, but love him she did, regardless. No use in hiding from it any longer. Only where Craig was concerned, nothing had changed. All he had proved was that he wanted her badly enough to take matters into his own hands.

As if sensing her regard, the grey eyes came open. Awareness was instantaneous. He smiled, lifting the arm from her waist to run his hand over her cheek in a gesture that brought faint hope to her heart.

'How do you feel?' he asked softly.

The words she wanted to say dried in her throat. They weren't what he would want to hear. 'Nowhere near as pleased with myself as you obviously feel,' she said thickly instead. 'You certainly proved how much of a man you are!'

The smile didn't so much fade as change character, while his eyes took on a harder glint. 'That's at least something.' His hand remained where it was, devoid now of tenderness—if there had been any to start with. 'You realise there's a good chance that we achieved what we're meant to achieve last night?'

'But still only a chance,' she returned, 'until it's proved otherwise.'

Craig levered himself up on an elbow, towering over her with a look of determination on his face. 'If you think I'm going to hang around until then, you can think again! If it didn't happen last night it's going to be given every opportunity from here on in. If you need some kind of moral support, you can always tell yourself you're only doing it for Charles!'

Rachel only just stopped herself from calling his name as he threw back the covers and leapt from the bed. There was no trace of self-consciousness in his nudity as he strode across to the bathroom. He looked what he was: a man of steel and purpose, ready to accept no compromise.

Last night had not been the product of a sudden uncontrollable urge, but a calculated assault on her senses with a view towards making it impossible for her to back out of the marriage. And there was every chance that he had won, because if she did turn out to be pregnant she would have no choice but to go through with it, if only to give the child legal status.

But only if she turned out to be pregnant, she thought with new if hollow resolution. And no further chances would be taken. From now on she would take care to lock her door at night.

CHAPTER SEVEN

BREAKFAST was an ordeal Rachel would willingly have forgone. With Caroline leaving today, however, she could come up with no reasonable-sounding excuse for her absence. A claim of illness would only bring the other to her door to see for herself, and she doubted her ability to act the part convincingly enough.

Dressed with careful aplomb in bright yellow shorts and sleeveless top, she made sure to be first down. Mother and son arrived together some few minutes later. Craig's expression revealed little of what he was thinking, as usual. For all the difference in his attitude, last night might never have happened.

'A nice day for travelling,' commented Caroline with reference to the continuing sunshine. 'When it comes this early in the season, it makes you wonder if it's going to last through the summer. Not,' she added, 'that I'm going to be in the country for a great part of it. I'm off to take stock of our Far East market in July.' She cast a glance at her son seated opposite. 'I suppose there's little chance of your having even a first draft ready before then?'

'I suppose you're right,' he returned equably. 'Maybe by the time you get back.'

'Something to look forward to.' She gave Rachel a smile which failed to warm. 'Along with other news, perhaps?'

'You never know,' was all Rachel allowed herself. She didn't even glance in Craig's direction. Let him make what he would of that statement. He couldn't force her into marriage. Only one thing could do that now.

It was Caroline herself who suggested a walk down to the beach before lunch. It was the last chance she was likely to have of feeling sand between her toes for some time, she said humorously. Rachel's attempt to cry off by reason of having some phone calls to make was turned aside with the brisk rejoinder that there was the whole afternoon to do that. It was too fine a morning to spend indoors, in any case, Caroline added by way of a clincher to the argument.

The latter kept on the casual skirt and lightweight sweater she was already wearing, simply changing her heeled shoes for a pair of stylish but more practical flatties. Craig came down in white shorts and T-shirt, with well-worn leather sandals on his feet.

'Holiday weather calls for holiday gear,' he declared lightly. 'It's been some time since I last felt sand between my toes, too.'

His mother gave him a glance which caused Rachel to wonder briefly if there was some hidden meaning in the remark. Reading too much into too little, she decided. What possible significance could there be apart from the obvious?

She forged ahead of the other two as they crossed the cliff-top meadow. The herd of yearling bullocks grazing there demonstrated their usual curiosity, flocking round her like jostling schoolboys. There had been a time when their size and clumsy playfulness would have unnerved her. Now, she simply waved a hand at them and tapped a couple of muzzles thrust too close, sending the owners skittering away in pretended nervousness.

'I'll buy you a cape for next time,' commented Craig satirically, as he and Caroline came up behind her. 'You came close to being trampled underfoot just there.'

'They're harmless,' Rachel claimed. 'Just looking for fun.'

'I suppose they don't have much else left in life,' said Caroline drily. 'Thank your lucky stars you weren't born a bull, Craig! It seems very few are left intact.'

'If the feminist movement gets its way, there won't be a great deal of difference,' he responded, equally drily. 'We're being emasculated right, left and centre!'

Rachel kept her gaze fixed steadfastly on the horizon. The remark had been aimed her way, she knew, but she wasn't going to allow it to get to her. Emasculated? That was some joke! Locked doors were her only defence.

Protected from the off-shore breeze, the little bay was warm enough for sunbathing. Caroline took off her shoes and tights and went for a paddle in the wavelets breaking on to the gently sloping shore. Salt-water was an excellent toner for the feet, she claimed.

Rachel joined her because the only alternative was to wait with Craig, who had declined the invitation. He sat on a rock a little way up the beach to watch the pair of them, one leg lifted across the other knee in an attitude that somehow gripped Rachel by the throat.

How could he be so casual after all that had happened between them last night? she thought numbly. Did it really mean so little to him? He had made love to other women in his time; perhaps it was her degree of response that fell short? And yet what else could he have expected of her? Recalling even snippets of detail to mind sent heat running through her. She had acted like someone possessed!

'You're very quiet this morning,' commented Caroline. 'Something bothering you?'

'No more than yesterday,' Rachel lied. She sought for some topic that didn't centre on Craig. 'You've never mentioned your other son while you've been here. Do you see much of him?'

'Considering we both work in the same city, not a lot,' came the apparently untroubled reply. 'He has his own lifestyle, I have mine. We meet up on high days and holidays, and occasionally have lunch together.'

Rachel said hesitantly, 'Does he know about... all this?'

'Only that Craig stands to inherit half the estate; not the rest.'

'How did he take it?'

Caroline shrugged. 'How would you expect? As the younger son, he stood in Craig's shadow for years before he struck out for himself. His career hit a bad patch recently, along with many others, so he hardly views his exclusion from the will with indifference. Craig might feel in a position to tide him over the hump until things start picking up again, if he could be sure he was going to inherit himself.' The pause was significant. 'It all rests with you.'

Rachel clenched her teeth down hard on the too hasty reply, and said instead, 'Craig doesn't come across as exactly short of money now.'

'That rather depends on one's concept of wealth. He's earned every penny of what he has, and I personally see no reason why he should be expected to pull Gary out of the mire at the cost of his own security. The favour certainly wouldn't be reciprocated were the boot on the other foot.'

'In which case, *I* see no reason to allow Gary's problems to influence *me*.' Rachel stepped free of the lapping waves to pick up the sandals she had discarded. 'I don't know about you,' she said over a shoulder, 'but I've had enough for today. I ordered an early lunch so you'd have plenty of time to make the ferry.'

'Can't wait to get rid of me, can you?' came the caustic rejoinder as the other followed her example. 'You won't find Craig so easy to dispatch.'

Rachel could have told her she already knew that, but she kept her own counsel. Whatever happened, it was between her and Craig alone—no one else.

He got to his feet as they came up the beach towards him. He even produced a couple of handkerchiefs for them to wipe their feet free of the clinging sand before donning footwear again.

'It's called being prepared for all eventualities,' he said with irony when Rachel thanked him for the gesture. 'I was a Boy Scout once. Ready to go back, are we?'

'Needs must, it seems,' answered his mother. 'An early lunch in preparation for an early departure.'

Rachel swamped any slight sense of shame beneath self-justification. Caroline's presence had only served to inflame the situation. At a swift calculation, she had almost two weeks to wait before she could be sure of her condition; even then, the concern alone might throw her cycle into disarray. Until she was sure, she was going to try not to dwell on things too much. Not the easiest of tasks, but then, nothing about this whole affair was easy.

The three of them parted, when they reached the house, in order to go and change. Sliding into a simple figured cotton dress in her favourite blues, Rachel wished, not for the first time, that she had some kind of regular occupation. It was doubtful now that Craig

would want her help; nor, if it came to that, did she feel
like working with him on this book. Offering to help
her mother in the shop was one solution, she supposed,
although not necessarily an offer the latter would jump
at. They had subtly yet surely grown apart this last couple
of years.

The knock on the door, followed by Craig's immediate entry into the room without waiting for an
answer, brought Rachel swinging round from the mirror
in heart-jerking consternation. It hadn't occurred to her
to turn the key in the lock in broad daylight.

'Did you ever hear of common courtesy?' she flung
at him, taking refuge in anger. 'Or is that a dirty word
where you come from?'

His shrug made light of the attack. 'It seemed unlikely I'd see anything I haven't already seen. We'll be
sharing the same room after we're married, anyway.'

'We're not going to be married.' She said it between
gritted teeth. 'Not unless——'

'Unless it turns out to be strictly necessary?' he supplied for her as she broke off. 'That's one reason,
certainly.'

'The *only* one,' she insisted, and saw his shoulders lift
again.

'I'm not about to enter into any verbal argument. I
came to suggest that you come to Ryde with us, then we
could go on to Cowes and take a look at the boats. If
we're going to sell the yacht, we'll need an independent
valuation.'

'We're in no position to consider selling as yet,' Rachel
rejoined. 'So there's not much point.'

'All the same, I'd like to take a look.' The strong
mouth had an inflexible cast. 'Better, surely, than moping

around the house for the rest of the afternoon, waiting
for me to get back?'

There was some sense in that, Rachel was forced to
acknowledge. 'All right,' she heard herself agreeing
without conscious intention, 'I'll come.'

'Good.' He hadn't moved further than the open door,
standing there with a hand still resting on the knob. 'And
tonight we're going out to dinner. Just the two of us for
once.'

'Candle-lit, of course?' she mocked, eliciting no more
than a brief smile.

'What's life without a little romance? Are you ready
to go down? Lunch should be just about on the table.'

With her hair obviously brushed and lipstick freshly
applied, there was no excuse she could find for further
delay. She nodded curtly, and preceded him from the
room, half anticipating some form of physical contact,
and aware of an unwarranted sense of deflation when it
didn't occur. Nothing about Craig Lindhurst was predictable; she was only just beginning to register that fact.

They left the house at one-fifteen to drive the few miles
across to Ryde. Rachel said her goodbyes to Caroline in
the car, leaving Craig to see his mother out to the pass-
enger-portal on his own. If they ever met again it would
be because matters had been taken out of her hands, she
thought, watching the two of them walk away from the
vehicle. Should it happen that way, she would hardly be
in a position to deny the other access to her son's home.

Craig returned some ten minutes later to slide behind
the wheel of the Mercedes without a word. If he was
angry because she hadn't made the effort to see his
mother off, that was too bad, Rachel told herself de-
fensively. She was making no concessions.

The boats were berthed at West Cowes, which meant a detour through Newport in order to cross the river. Rachel hated passing the prison. The very thought of being locked away for years on end was enough to bring her out in a cold sweat.

'It doesn't seem all that much of a deterrent to some,' Craig observed when she said as much. 'Anyway, it's unlikely to happen to you—unless you commit some serious crime, that is.' He added with irony, 'So if you're considering keeping a knife handy, I'd think again. Crimes of passion aren't regarded with any sympathy in this country.'

'Self-defence is,' Rachel retorted.

His laugh was short. 'From what? I'm hardly out to kill you.'

The whole conversation was ridiculous, and she knew it, but something in her refused to let it go. 'Death before dishonour might be an outmoded concept where you're concerned, but there are those of us who still think it holds some merit!'

'A bit on the late side, wouldn't you say?' He was definitely amused now, mouth curving. 'To coin a phrase, it's time to lie back and enjoy it.'

Her eyes went instinctively to the lean hands on the wheel, recalling with tremoring clarity the havoc they had wreaked on her in the night. The churning inside her at the thought of repetition had nothing to do with fear.

'Let's agree to shelve the whole subject for the time being,' Craig suggested after a moment or two when she failed to come up with any smart rejoinder. He sounded just a little weary of it himself. 'We're going to look over the boats, have tea somewhere and enjoy a few hours free of friction. OK?'

Temporary measure or no, Rachel seized on the olive-branch as a means of getting through the rest of the day. 'OK.'

The truce worked quite well for a time. Showing Craig over the yacht Charles had loved, she felt no more than the odd pang or two. Craig himself proved knowledgeable enough on the subject of sailing in general, but reiterated his lack of interest in racing.

'Apart from the odd game of tennis or maybe squash, competitive sports leave me cold,' he confessed. 'I'm a lousy cricketer, and rugby's for idiots.'

'How about football?' asked Rachel lightly, and elicited a smile from Craig.

'I don't cry convincingly either.' Running a hand over the smooth teak of the hatch cover, he added casually, 'What about you? I know you swim well, but do you have any other sporting interests?'

'Like you, I suppose,' she admitted. 'Tennis and squash mostly. Charles had plans to put in a hard court before he——' She broke off, shaking her head ruefully. 'I didn't mean to bring his name up.'

Craig had his gaze fixed on a craft just pulling out. 'Why not? He was your husband, after all.'

'A fact you still view with repugnance,' she stated flatly.

'Aversion, maybe.' His voice had hardened. 'The thought of you and him doing what we did last night——'

'We didn't!' It was out before she could stop it, before she could even think about it. She saw the dark head swing sharply towards her, and made some attempt to straighten out the impression. 'I mean, not like that. Charles wasn't . . . he didn't . . .' She stopped, hot colour staining her skin at the sardonic lift of his brow.

'Never summoned quite the same degree of response, is that what you're trying to say? I gathered that much for myself.'

'How?' The question was dragged from her.

'The way you reacted. You weren't accustomed to letting go with such totality—you even fought it at first. Making love with a father figure erects all kinds of barriers in the mind.'

'I suppose you hold a degree in psychology too?' Rachel derided caustically.

'I don't need any degree to see what stares me in the face.' Craig took her by the shoulders, forcing her to look at him. 'You married Charles because he represented the security you lost when your father died. Someone you could lean on, rely on to take care of you. Love of a kind, I'll grant you.'

'I suppose it's marginally better than just wanting him for his money,' she got out, hardly able to speak at all through the lump in her throat. 'You have to be right, don't you, Craig? You can't accept that a man of sixty could possibly hold any normal kind of attraction for someone my age, so you denigrate it. Well, listen, and listen hard. I loved Charles the way I'll never love anyone else. The way you and your kind couldn't even begin to appreciate!'

Her voice took on strength and purpose as the anger and resentment grew in her. 'You see love as synonymous with sex, and you're very good at it. *I'll* grant *you* that much. Only there's a whole lot more to life than simple sexual pleasure!'

There was a spark in the grey eyes, though whether of anger or amusement she couldn't be sure. His response seemed to confirm the latter. 'So you do admit to getting pleasure from it?'

The lack of backlash took the wind completely out of her sails, and left her floundering. She looked at him helplessly, unable to come up with the withering retort she craved.

'I'll take that as a "yes",' he said, and kissed her, running both hands into her hair to mould the back of her head in a manner that allowed her no retreat.

Her protest, such as it was, lasted bare seconds before giving way to the rising tide of heat through her veins. Her pulses were racing, her whole body tremoring to the memory of where his kisses could lead. The domination of mind over matter was a joke where this was concerned. She could no more stop herself responding to him than fly!

More than half anticipating a move to take her below, she was momentarily bewildered when he put her away from him, and could only stand there gazing at him with darkened eyes.

'It will keep,' he said. 'We still have the dinghy to look at. Supposing we do that?'

It was the sheer calculation that hurt so much, Rachel told herself dully. He knew exactly how far to go to have her dancing to his tune. Loving a man of his kind was futile, in the sense that he was incapable of returning the emotion, but there was no backing away from it. Different from what she had felt for Charles by a mile, different from anything she had ever felt for anyone. It was possible to hate and love at the same time, and she was the living proof.

She managed to regain some semblance of self-possession during the following hour or so. There was no way, she vowed, that she was going to let Craig guess how she really felt about him. Her bedroom door would be locked the moment she retired for the night, and it would stay that way. It was only in the deepest recesses of her mind that she acknowledged a hope for her pregnancy to be confirmed and give her the excuse she needed to retreat from her sworn position.

By tacit consent they gave tea a miss. Craig seemed determined to keep the atmosphere light on the way back to Apperknowle.

'I rang through to the garage handling my car earlier,' he remarked at one point. 'It'll be ready for collection tomorrow. As you can't run me in, I'll have to surrender a principle and let Grayson take me.' He paused before tagging on casually, 'Have you thought any more about learning to drive?'

Rachel shrugged and shook her head. 'Not a great deal.' She added with deliberation, 'I suppose it wouldn't be a bad idea, though. Grayson stands to lose his job anyway if the estate goes under the hammer, and I'd hardly be in position to keep on a chauffeur myself.'

Craig drove for a moment in silence, mouth taut. 'You just don't let go, do you?' he stated grimly. 'What exactly are you trying to get me to say?'

'Nothing at all,' she denied with a bland intonation she hadn't planned on, and didn't particularly care for, yet seemed somehow unable to alter. 'I was under the impression you'd already said all there was to say.'

They were running through Brighstone Forest, with no other traffic in sight at present. Craig drew up at the roadside, where the trees crowded thickly, to sit gazing through the windscreen with an oddly bleak look on his face. Uncertain of his mood, and already regretting the resumption of hostilities, Rachel watched him from the corner of her eye. He had at least been making some effort to keep matters on a reasonably congenial level. Why did she have to spoil it?

'If I thought that taking you in there, ripping your clothes off, and showing you what pure animal instinct is really like would do any good, I'd do it,' he said on a low, rough note. 'It isn't just sex I want from you. I could get that anywhere, for God's sake!'

'Do you think I don't know that?' she asked huskily. 'Do you think I don't realise how far I am from being the kind of woman you're used to having around? You didn't get to know what you know without lots of experience, while I've only known one other man. I can't offer the degree of satisfaction you're accustomed to.'

The grey eyes studied her with narrowed intent. 'You're not listening. I just got through saying it isn't just sexual satisfaction I'm looking for. Not that you don't provide it. Last night was as good for me as I'm fairly sure it was for you.' He brought up a hand to cup her face, smoothing the line of her lips with the ball of his thumb. 'You're a beautiful, sensual, wholly desirable young woman, and I'd be a liar if I said that didn't have any bearing; but there's more to it than that.'

Rachel was trembling like a leaf inside, possessed of an almost overwhelming urge to give in to the emotions flooding her and let him have his way regardless. It was only a tiny part of her that stood fast, but it was an ungovernable part.

'Such as Apperknowle and what goes with it?' she suggested with only the faintest of quivers in her voice. 'I'm not a fool, Craig. You wouldn't even be here if it weren't for the will!'

The thumb had stopped moving; for a brief moment it trembled on the brink of applying a pressure designed to hurt. His eyes were pure ice, his voice cutting.

'Perfectly true. I wouldn't even have known you existed, except as a name. As you're so sure of my motives, it's obviously a waste of time arguing the toss any further on the score, so I'll simply settle for what I'm due.' He shook his head as she made to speak. 'Don't bother telling me it isn't going to happen, because I've no intention of accepting it. You gave Charles your word, remember—or doesn't that mean anything to you any more?'

'Of course it does!' Her face was pale, her whole body numb.

'Then you'll keep it. And not in six months either. If there's any chance at all of your being pregnant, and there is, then we should make it legitimate as of now. If what people might say matters so much to you, we can be married on the mainland and keep the whole thing a secret until such time as you feel able to announce it. An ordinary licence and a register office is all we'll need. Portsmouth should do.'

'Stop it!' Rachel could hardly believe he was really serious. 'Just stop it!'

'No way. I'll go over and make the arrangements to-morrow after I collect the car. You can come if you want to, though it isn't strictly necessary. Your signature will only be required on the day.'

She sat frozen as he fired the ignition with a flick of a lean brown wrist, unable to find a single thing to say. It wasn't going to be like that, of course, because she wouldn't allow it; but she couldn't defy the challenge he had flung at her either. Marry him, or deny Charles his last request—that was her only choice. Which left her with no choice at all in the end.

No further word passed between them during the following minutes. On reaching the house, Craig drove the Mercedes straight round to the garage courtyard, bringing it to a jerky halt to sit for a seemingly stunned moment gazing at the red Porsche already parked there. The expletive was under his breath, but no less savage for it.

'Who is it?' Rachel was moved to ask.

'My brother,' came the abrupt reply. 'No need to wonder what he's doing here!'

Grayson appeared from one of the garages as they got out of the car. He had a polishing-cloth in his hand.

'Mr Lindhurst arrived about an hour ago,' he confirmed in answer to Craig's query. 'Came over on the two o'clock to Fishbourne, he said.' He paused. 'Shall I garage the Porsche, sir?'

Craig shook his head. 'He won't be staying.'

Rachel waited until they were inside the house before making any contribution. 'You can hardly expect him to turn right round and go back tonight!'

'Why not?' came the curt rejoinder. 'He came unexpectedly, he can leave the same way. The last thing I need right now is Gary on my back!'

They had reached the hall. The man lounging in the library doorway regarded the pair of them with a pained expression. He was as fair as Craig was dark, and handsome in a devil-may-care kind of way that suited his flamboyant red shirt and white hipster trousers.

'Some welcome, even from you, dear brother! And after travelling for five traffic-laden hours to get here!' The smile lurking in his eyes as he switched his attention to Rachel belied his plaintive tone. 'Hi there! I'm Gary, if you haven't already guessed. I thought it was time I met my new aunt.'

It was the very first time that she had ever considered the relationship. If she was Gary's aunt by marriage, then she was Craig's too. The thought was intriguing enough to elicit a smile of her own, albeit a faint one.

'Hello, Gary,' she said. 'Nice to see you.'

'Nice to know I'm welcomed by someone.' He looked back at his brother, whose expression hadn't relaxed at all. 'Sorry if I chose a bad time, but I had a few days' holiday to use up before the end of April, and thought I'd take advantage of the weather. Mother still here, is she?'

'You knew damned well she was leaving today, or you wouldn't be here,' Craig clipped.

'True, I suppose.' Gary neither sounded nor looked repentant. 'Anyway, seeing I am here, couldn't we stop playing Cain and Abel for once, and try being sociable?'

'Why don't the two of you go and chat in the library while I see about tea?' suggested Rachel diplomatically before Craig could form a reply. 'Say ten minutes?'

Craig scarcely spared her a glance. 'Fine.'

Gary stepped back from the doorway as his brother approached. Craig closed the door behind him once he was through, leaving Rachel to go and do as she had offered. With the tea organised, she took the opportunity to slip upstairs and run a brush through her wind-tangled hair.

There were dark shadows under her eyes, she noted in the mirror. Hardly surprising after the stress of the last hour. In many ways, she was grateful for Gary's arrival. It gave her breathing-space. If she had anything at all to do with it, he would be staying on for a while. She needed him.

CHAPTER EIGHT

GARY looked somewhat less buoyant when Rachel finally joined the two brothers.

'Seems it's to be flying visit,' he said wryly. 'I've had my marching orders.'

Rachel forbore from so much as glancing in Craig's direction. Her smile felt fixed, though her voice was level enough. 'You're welcome to stay as long as you like, Gary. It might be some time before we have another opportunity to get to know one another. I've already told Mrs Brantley. She'll have a room ready for you by the time we finish tea.'

'Well, thanks!' He was obviously delighted. He cast a sly glance at his brother, whose face had acquired a granite-like set. 'I can hardly turn down an invitation like that.'

'No,' came the brusque agreement, 'I'm sure you can't. I'll leave the two of you to exchange life-stories.'

Rachel knew a momentary regret as he went from the room. Whatever the source of the antagonism between the two, she wasn't helping by stepping into the breach. On the other hand, she reassured herself, it wasn't her place to take sides either, any more than it was Craig's place to assume that much authority without so much as a by-your-leave.

'I won't ask why you're at cross purposes,' she said. 'That's between you and Craig. Tea will be here any minute. Why don't we sit down and wait for it?'

The smile was designed to charm. 'Why not? And, just for the record, the cross purposes are all on Craig's side. I came to congratulate him—and to meet you, of course—whereas he thinks I'm only here to sound out future prospects.'

'Prospects of what?' she asked, drawn despite herself.

'Financial backing.' He gave a rueful grimace. 'I'm not doing any too well at present, admittedly, but asking him for money was the last thing on my mind.'

Rachel hesitated before voicing the question. 'Then you don't feel any resentment because Charles only named Craig in his will?'

Gary laughed. 'Well, I wouldn't go so far as to deny a slight pique. After all, there's more than enough of it to go round. Not,' he tagged on swiftly, 'that I'm including your own half of the estate. You're more than entitled.'

'Thank you.' There was just the faintest trace of irony in her voice. 'Did you ever come to Apperknowle before?'

'I was never invited.' He stretched out comfortably in the deep armchair, his gaze appraising as it swept the room. 'Uncle Charles kept himself very much to himself where the family was concerned. He and my father were estranged, you know. Dad was another who got left out in the cold.'

'Not entirely, surely?'

'Comparatively speaking. Charles inherited the bulk of the estate. All Dad got was a lump sum.'

'Couldn't he have appealed for a fairer division through the courts?' Rachel ventured.

'Too proud. Family tradition favours the elder son. Always has, probably always will.'

Not, Rachel vowed, if she had anything to do with it. Any children of hers would be treated with total equality—male *or* female!

She brought herself up short on that thought. She didn't even have the one child yet!

Gary was looking at her with speculative expression. 'You're very different from what I expected,' he observed candidly. 'I thought you'd be one of those Page-Three types old men usually go for.'

'Charles wasn't old,' Rachel disputed for what seemed like the millionth time. 'If you look as good as he did at sixty, you'll be lucky!'

The grin held no hint of apology. 'If I live to be sixty I'll be past caring. At least you're young enough to start over—and with the looks for it, too. Were it not for the fact that you'd think I was only after your money, I'd propose to you myself right here and now!'

It was impossible to be angry with him, Rachel conceded, unable to restrain a smile. After what she had gone through with Craig this afternoon, it was sheer relief to have humour take a hand.

'Were it not for the fact that I'm inclined to agree with you, I might even consider it,' she returned flippantly. She turned as the door opened on the rattle of crockery. 'Here's tea.'

Pert and pretty in her black and white, Doreen viewed the new addition to the household with an interest returned in full.

'Nice,' commented Gary approvingly on her departure, not bothering to wait until the door was closed. 'I must say, I like the set-up here. Waited on hand and foot—who could want for more?' He took the cup Rachel handed him, and drank from it before setting it down. 'Has Craig said what he plans to do with his time now he's able to pick and choose? I imagine he might feel like taking things easy after what happened out there.' Catching her change of expression, he gave her a suddenly sharper scrutiny. 'You do know about his desert sojourn?'

'No,' Rachel admitted. 'He doesn't talk about his work.'

'The strong, silent type, that's my brother! He was taken prisoner by guerrillas and held hostage for close to eight months. Apparently, conditions were pretty rough, and he was generally given a bad time of it. I don't know all the details myself, only what I've managed to glean from Mother. The two of them are pretty close, as you might have noticed.'

'Yes.' Rachel was silent for a moment or two, going over what she had just learned. 'How come they let him go in the end? Was a ransom paid, or something?'

Gary shook his head. 'Seems he escaped. Walked forty miles with only a single canteen of water. Must have been hell in that kind of heat. I guess you have to admire his guts. It isn't the first time he's been in trouble. He narrowly escaped an ambush in Beirut a couple of years back. A risk I wouldn't take myself, I don't mind admitting. There's no news story worth it.'

'Craig must have thought there was.' Rachel was still trying to come to terms with the sense of shame. He had gone through all that only to come home to...this. If only she had known.

'So it seems. A real lionheart!' There was a certain sardonic edge in the declaration. 'He'll be a fool to carry on, though—especially when he doesn't need to. His luck is bound to run out some time.'

Some luck! Rachel thought ironically. Eight months of sheer horror from the sound of it, never knowing when he might be released, or even if he ever would be released, subjected to affronts she couldn't even begin to realise. Such an experience would have broken a lesser man. Craig had not only survived in body, but in mind too. It said a whole lot for his character.

Knowing what she did now, she couldn't hate him any more. Hate was the wrong word for what she felt anyway. It wasn't his fault that he didn't return the same depth of emotion. Wanting her the way he so obviously did was enough to be going on with. They could make a go of this marriage if they worked at it. A baby might even help. Men were notoriously proud to have proof of their virility.

'Are you still with me?' asked Gary curiously. 'You look as if you just made some soul-shaking discovery!'

Rachel summoned a smile and a dismissive shrug. 'Something I forgot to do, that's all. More tea, or would you like to see where you'll be sleeping?'

'No, thanks, and yes, please,' he said. 'I could use a shower and a change of clothes.' He got to his feet along with her. 'You'll be here for dinner?'

Recalling Craig's stated intention, Rachel hesitated to commit herself. It was unlikely, though, that he would still be considering taking her out after the way she had gone against him. She had a lot of making up to do, and very little idea of where to start. The sooner the better, she supposed.

'Yes,' she acknowledged. 'We normally eat around eight, but feel free to help yourself to a drink if you're down before anyone else. Just make yourself at home, Gary.'

'Thanks,' he said. 'I will.'

Mrs Brantley had remade the bed in the room Caroline had occupied. Rachel left Gary at the door with a reiterated injunction to feel at home. She hesitated outside Craig's bedroom door, nerving herself to knock. The lack of reply brought mixed feelings. If he was in there and ignoring the summons, it could only be because he was too furious with her to want to talk to her. Except that he wouldn't know it was her at the door, would he? Which seemed to suggest that he might be elsewhere in the house, or even had gone out again.

Easier if she left things as they were for the moment, she concluded. There would be time enough to convey her change of heart later.

She found Gary already comfortably ensconced in the drawing-room when she went down. He cast an admiring eye over the calf-length burgundy dress which fitted her slender curves so well.

'You're a sight for sore eyes, milady!' he exclaimed.

'I'd as soon you didn't call me that, even in a joke,' she said lightly. 'So far as I'm concerned, the title died with Charles. I'm just plain Mrs.'

'Not so plain,' he returned irrepressibly. 'In fact, downright fetching! I can't blame Uncle Charles for going overboard. Where did Craig get to, I wonder? I've been downstairs nearly an hour, and haven't seen hide nor hair of him. You don't think he's sulking in his room because you stood up for me, by any chance?'

'Don't be ridiculous!' Her tone was sharper than she had intended; she made an effort to soften it. 'Sulking isn't one of your brother's traits. He'll be here in his own good time.'

'Master of the house, and all that—well, half the house, at any rate.' The deceptively lazy hazel eyes glinted at her. 'You two should get married and bring it together. Probably what Charles intended should happen. The luck of the devil, that brother of mine! All this and you too!

I'd give him some competition if I had anything substantial to offer.' His glance went past her to the door. 'Speaking of the devil...'

If Craig heard the comment he gave no indication. Clad in dark trousers and silky roll-necked sweater, he looked composed and devastatingly attractive. The eyes briefly meeting Rachel's were devoid of expression.

'I cancelled the reservation,' he said. 'That is what you wanted?'

'I thought you said you didn't have any other arrangement?' put in Gary before she could answer. 'You didn't have to cancel because of little old me. I'd have been right as rain on my own.'

'It wasn't important.' Rachel could have kicked herself the moment she had said it. She didn't dare look at Craig again. 'There's always another night,' she hastened to add.

'Plenty,' Craig agreed drily. 'I see you found a drink, Gary. What will you have, Rachel?'

'Surprise me,' she invited, surprising herself with the unintended coquettishness in the words. It was too late to retract without making a total fool of herself, so she followed it with a smile that drew a lift of one dark eyebrow.

'As you like,' he said.

Gary viewed the flags raised in her cheeks with a suddenly thoughtful look in his eyes. Rachel could almost hear the cogs going round. Not that it really mattered any more if he guessed how things were. Some time this evening, if she could get him alone, she planned on telling Craig she would definitely marry him, although not quite as soon as he had said, unless things worked out that way.

Finding a reason for her decision which didn't include giving herself away completely was going to be the most difficult part. Telling him she loved him would only complicate matters because he couldn't, in honesty, return the compliment. Better to let him believe she was doing it for Charles. For now, anyway.

He brought her a sherry on the rocks, handing over the glass with a look in his eye that challenged her to complain. Sipping it, she had to acknowledge that the Americans weren't total philistines; it tasted different, true, but it was good.

Seating himself at her side on the brocade sofa, he took a swallow from his own glass before turning a level gaze on his brother.

'Since you're going to be here for a while, I should point out that you'll have to entertain yourself for the most part. Rachel and I have some business to take care of in Portsmouth tomorrow, after which she's agreed to give me a hand sorting out my notes.'

'Notes on what?' Gary queried.

'The book I'm going to be writing.'

'Is that a fact?' The younger man sounded torn between derision and rancour. 'I suppose Mother's going to see it published?'

'Providing it meets her criteria. She draws an immovable line where professional judgement comes into play, as you very well know.'

'Oh, it will. You always were a wordsmith. Did you ever read any of his stuff?' The last to Rachel.

She shook her head. 'I'm afraid not. I never seemed to have time in the past to do more than just skim through a newspaper.'

'You missed out. His byline is known the world over. Trouble and strife in all its graphic glory!' Gary took a large swig of whisky. 'I'd expected to see a centre-page spread on your latest story by now—or are you saving it for the book?'

'The idea for that took shape beforehand,' came the unmoved reply. 'If it takes off there'll most likely be others, so who knows? Anyway, there are better things to talk about.'

'I took the liberty of filling Rachel in on the detail,' Gary continued with cool deliberation. 'She was most impressed!'

'You don't know the damned detail!' Craig was suddenly blazingly angry, and making no attempt to conceal it. 'No one does!'

Gary showed no sign of backing down. 'Only as much as you told Mother, admittedly, and peeling that from her was some job. Why the reticence, anyhow? You're a regular hero to us ordinary mortals. Given the same circumstances, I'd have just thrown in my lot with the rebels!'

'Time to go through for dinner,' put in Rachel hastily, frightened that Craig was about to rise and smite the younger man with the fist he had clenched. 'Cook will be devastated if we let her soup go cold!'

'What, no gong?' queried Gary on a satirical note.

'No butler either,' she returned with determined flippancy. 'Not quite far enough up the social scale.'

His grin applauded the come-back. 'Quick-witted too. Quite a combination!'

Craig was on his feet and in full command of himself again, although there was no disguising the hard set of his jaw. 'Let's eat,' he said stonily.

It was left to Rachel to keep the cart on the wheels during the rest of the interminable evening. Gary seemed bent on goading his brother into losing control of his temper—seemed almost to have a purpose in it, in fact. It rather put paid to Craig's theory that he was there to ask for money; had there been any chance to start with, Gary had fouled it up himself.

She was relieved when the time finally came when she could plausibly plead tiredness. With some trepidation, she left the two men to make their own farewells. They were both adults; she could hardly play mediator all night.

There had been no opportunity to speak with Craig on his own, yet there was a need in her to have things sorted that was going to make sleep difficult to come by. A part of her hoped that he would come straight to her room when he finally took his leave of his brother. Hearing his familiar footsteps pass her door some twenty minutes later brought a despondency hard to shake off. If he wouldn't come to her, she would have to go to him, she resolved in the end. It couldn't be left like this. Not now.

He was only three doors away. Her tentative knock brought no immediate response; she had to repeat it before he came. He was already undressed, and wearing a Paisley silk robe. From the bareness of his legs, she gathered that he was naked beneath it.

'I need to talk to you,' she said huskily. '*Just* talk, Craig.'

His lips twisted. 'What else?' He opened the door wider. 'You'd better come in.'

It was the first time she had been in the room since the day he had arrived. Little more than a week ago, she realised with a sense of shock. Falling in love with a man in that short length of time was precipitate under any circumstances.

His back against the solid mahogany, he surveyed her with almost clinical appraisal. 'So what was it you wanted to say?'

'Only that I'd decided to go ahead with the marriage,' she announced with a fair degree of assurance. She searched the lean features, looking for something she knew she wasn't going to find. 'That is what you want, isn't it?'

'It's what Charles wanted,' he rejoined. 'Why the sudden change of heart? Only this afternoon you were still looking for an out.'

'I've had time to think things through since then,' she claimed. 'You were right; I can't go back on my word to Charles. In any case——' She broke off, biting her lip as his expression altered.

'In any case—what? Are you finally going to admit you actually want me?' He came away from the door to take her chin in his hand and tilt her face towards him, eyes penetrating her defences. 'So say it. I want to hear the words plain and clear, so there'll be no misunderstandings. *Say* it!'

'I want you.' Her voice was low and shaky, but not indistinct. 'You already know that!'

'Knowing is one thing, having it confirmed another.' Face and voice had mellowed. 'I'm glad you finally grew up, Rachel. We can start to build on it now.'

She went into his arms without protest, eager for his lips on hers, for the possessive touch of his hands. Only when both kisses and caresses began to accelerate did she reluctantly draw back from him.

'I don't think we should take any more chances, Craig. Not until after the wedding.'

'It's only going to be a few days,' he said. 'What difference will it make?' His tone roughened again. 'If you weren't prepared to indulge the inclination, you should have stayed away. I'm in no mood for playing teasing games!'

Rachel stiffened instinctively, then forced herself to relax. 'I'm *not* teasing you,' she denied. 'I wouldn't do that. Not after all you've been through!'

He went very still, face suddenly blanked of all expression. The grey eyes were flinty. 'I'm not sure what Gary told you, but the last damn thing I need is consoling. Going without a woman was the least of it!'

'I didn't mean it like that,' she protested. 'I really didn't, Craig!' She caught at his arm as he made to turn away, dragging him back round with a strength born of desperation. 'I came because I wanted to tell you I'd made up my mind, that's all. If consolation were all I had planned, I'd be providing it right now.'

He studied her for a long and contemplative moment, eyes narrowed, then nodded. 'All right, I'll buy that. I just don't need sympathy.'

'How about empathy?' she asked softly. 'I'd like to think I could at least try to appreciate what it was like out there. You didn't even tell your mother all of it, did you?'

'I told her as much as she needed to know,' he said. 'I'd as soon forget the rest, if I'm allowed to.'

'But can you?' Rachel insisted. 'Is bottling it all up really going to help in the long run? Perhaps it might be a good thing to do as Gary suggested, and put it all down on paper.'

'Perhaps the two of you should go into partnership as psychologists,' came the short reply. 'I don't need to talk about it, I don't need to write about it, and I certainly don't need counselling by some kid scarcely out of nappies. Clear?'

The hurt was like a knife-wound. 'As crystal!' she jerked back. 'I'll leave you to it.'

He caught hold of her as she made to pass him, holding her fast when she struggled to free herself. There was a rueful look in his eyes. 'That was uncalled for. I'm sorry.'

She subsided at once, looking at him uncertainly. 'I didn't intend to pry. You're entitled to your privacy.'

His smile was brief. 'On the other hand, you may well be right about bottling it up.' He paused, seemed to gather himself. 'You know the gist of it already. I was held in several different camps. When they shifted me from one to another it was in neck and ankle-chains, slave fashion, tied behind a horse. I didn't go hungry—once my system accustomed itself to food I wouldn't have given a stray dog—or particularly thirsty either. They needed to keep me in reasonably good physical shape. I'd have been of no value dead.'

Rachel was silent, eyes riveted to his, dreading to hear more, yet reluctant to call a halt on something she herself had set into motion.

'The worst of it was the degradation,' he went on. 'Kept in rags, not allowed to wash—smelling my own filth! To them I was nothing but scum, so I could live like it.'

'Did they. . . torture you?' Rachel whispered.

'Only mentally. Not knowing when or even if it's going to end is torture enough. I'd be there still if they hadn't got careless. Either that or dead. I think they'd begun to realise I wasn't worth all that much as a bargaining measure. Anyway, that's about it. I'm here now, intact in mind and matter, so all ended well.'

She said wryly, 'Do you feel any better for having told me about it?'

He smiled and shrugged. 'I can't say I do. But then, I can't say I feel any worse for it either, so no harm done. The best thing we can both do now is forget it.'

He hadn't told her everything, Rachel was sure, nor probably ever would. He was right; it needed to be, if not forgotten, at least put aside.

'You'd better get to bed,' he said. 'I thought we'd go over to Portsmouth in the morning, then I can collect the Jag in the afternoon.'

It was beyond her at the moment to argue the point. All they were going to fix tomorrow was a licence. It didn't have to be used right away. Now that the moment had come, she didn't want to leave him, but any offer to stay would only be misconstrued.

'I'm sorry to have been so pig-headed about everything,' she proffered on impulse. Her smile was slow. 'Hyphenated, of course.'

Craig's answering smile had an edge. 'We reached an understanding in the end.' His kiss was cool and quick— too quick. 'See you in the morning.'

Rachel was outside the door before she released the pent-up breath. Holding it had been her only defence against telling him how she felt about him. It was too soon. Far too soon. He might take that as mere sympathy too.

Having Gary around wasn't going to improve matters, she acknowledged, yet she could hardly tell him to go now. It might even be as well to tell him the truth. He was going to have to know sooner or later. Only not the baby part of it, of course. That would hopefully come about as a seemingly normal circumstance of marriage itself.

Gary himself was in obvious high spirits at breakfast. He'd been for an early-morning swim, he said, and thoroughly enjoyed it.

'I might take myself off for a drive round the island while you're gone,' he announced. 'It's supposed to be worth seeing. When do you think you might be back?'

It was Craig who answered. 'Depends on how long it takes.'

'Well, I'll see you at dinner, if not before.' He sounded quite cheerful about it. 'I'm going to enjoy this break. The first one I've had in months! You two don't know how lucky you are not to be tied down to routine.'

'Oh, I think we do,' replied his brother levelly. 'And I agree; you may as well take advantage of it while you can.'

'Meaning it's likely to be the last chance I get?' Gary guessed on a slightly less buoyant note. 'Not just your say-so, though, is it?' The last with a glance in Rachel's direction. 'You're not going to pull in the welcome mat on me, are you, sweet aunt?'

'If you keep on calling me that, yes,' she said, wishing he would leave her out of it.

He put a hand over his heart in exaggerated sincerity. 'Never again, on my life!'

Craig made no further comment. Debating an issue yet to arise was a waste of time and effort, Rachel gathered from his shrug. Considering the fact that Gary was hardly going to be contemplating a regular to-ing and fro-ing, she couldn't see the point in making an issue of it here and now either. It would be something to talk about at a later date, after their own affairs were settled.

Wisely, Gary himself made no further reference to future visits. Dashing in pale blue trousers and gilet worn over a bright patterned shirt, he came out to wave the pair of them off when they left in the Mercedes at nine.

'As if he owned the place!' Craig observed drily, going down the drive. 'I'd as soon you didn't invite him to come again, if you don't mind.'

Rachel hesitated before voicing the question. 'Why is there such antagonism between you two? I realise you're totally different in temperament, but so are a lot of others.'

'There's only one person of importance in Gary's life,' came the terse response. 'The only time he ever bothers to contact Mother is when he wants something.'

'Does she contact him?'

'When she can. She leads a pretty busy life herself.'

Rachel could imagine. Caroline didn't come across as the deeply caring type either, for that matter. 'All the same,' she murmured, 'he is your only brother.'

'And blood is supposed to be thicker than water?' He shook his head. 'Doesn't mean a thing. You choose your friends on the basis of mutual liking and respect, so why should you feel bound to hold the same regard for those who've done nothing to merit it just because they happen to be related? Gary wouldn't turn a hair if I keeled over tomorrow. No, that's wrong. Under present circumstances, he'd expect to be next in line for a take-over.' He paused consideringly. 'Come to think of it, I don't recall any provision in the will regarding the event of my death prior to our completing the proviso.'

They were out on the lane now, and moving towards Brighstone to take the Shorwell to Newport road, sea and sky creating a straight-lined horizon to the right. 'I suppose,' Rachel said carefully, 'it would be a matter for the courts to decide. There are strict laws laid down for right of inheritance, aren't there?'

'Yes, there are. And, as the sale ruling only comes into force if we refuse to carry out the condition, then I imagine there'd be a good chance of Gary's being judged the rightful heir as the only surviving Lindhurst by birth.'

Rachel turned her head to study the strongly chiselled profile. 'You think he might have worked that out for himself?'

'And be planning to bump me off?' Craig said with a faint smile. 'We might not be close, but let's not get paranoid! In any case, he doesn't even know about the condition.'

'That's true.' She gave a little laugh. 'I didn't really consider it a possibility. He just isn't the type.'

Craig gave her a suddenly narrowed glance. 'You like him, don't you?'

It was a difficult question to answer in the circumstances. She sought for some adequate response. 'I can't totally dislike someone I hardly know. He's been nice enough to me so far.'

'Well, naturally. Any man would be.'

'I don't,' she said, 'remember you being all that impressed the first time we met.'

'Oh, I was.' This time the smile was wider. 'Just the circumstances made it a bit difficult to express. If I'd known then how far things were going to go between us, I might have seen you in a different light altogether. You hardly helped with that "keep-your-distance" attitude.'

'Self-defence,' Rachel claimed. 'How do you think I felt, knowing what I was going to have to tell you—a total stranger?'

'Not being a woman, it's hard to imagine,' he agreed. 'We have different outlooks. All *I* felt when I knew was that my stars must be in the ascendency. How many men get to acquire a beautiful young wife and a fortune at one and the same time? If you expected me to turn the offer down, you were barking up the wrong tree.'

'I didn't,' she admitted. 'Not really. To be honest, I'm not sure what I hoped for most. Keeping my word to Charles was important, of course, but——'

'Let's forget about your word to Charles, shall we?' Craig's tone was steady, his expression unrevealing. 'It's just the two of us now.'

Perhaps three, if the one night's indulgence proved to have positive results, thought Rachel wryly. She would be glad when she knew for sure.

CHAPTER NINE

THE catamaran crossing to Portsmouth proved both fast and comfortable. Combined with the proximity of the rail line on the mainland, it made commuting even to London a not too unreasonable proposition, as Craig observed.

Hardly the kind of thing he would be contemplating himself on a regular basis, Rachel reflected on a sombre note. His journalistic forays obviously ranged far and wide. Only if his first novel really took off might he consider altering his lifestyle long term. She would just have to live in hope.

Obtaining a licence proved no problem at all. It was possible, Rachel discovered, to purchase a combined certificate and licence which would enable a marriage to take place after only one clear working day. She wasn't quite sure whether to be relieved or otherwise when Craig made no attempt to suggest that they took advantage of it.

'You can relax for at least the next three weeks,' he said with faint irony on emerging from the register office. 'The certificate can't be issued now until notice of intent has been displayed for that length of time.'

Rachel cast a sharpened glance. 'You mean our names will be on display?'

'Only to anyone interested, which isn't likely to be many people. That, in case you'd forgotten, is why we're here in Portsmouth instead of Newport.'

'No, I hadn't forgotten.' She made a wry gesture. 'I just can't bear the thought of all the talk!'

Craig shrugged. 'People will talk whenever it becomes known. Something you're going to have to live with.'

Something she could manage to live with if only she had his love to support her, came the disconsolating thought. Only she hadn't, and wasn't likely to have, and must learn to accept that too.

They had lunch before taking the one p.m. sailing back to Ryde. With no one available to drive the Mercedes, it was necessary to return to Apperknowle before Craig could go and pick up the Jaguar, arriving there around two o'clock to find that Gary had appropriated both Grayson and the Rolls for his tour of the island.

'Typical,' Craig asserted furiously. 'So bloody typical! This settles it. He's leaving as soon as he gets back!'

'You can't just throw him out on his ear,' Rachel protested. 'Not after I told him he could stay. He obviously didn't think about you needing transport.' She paused, trying to find some appeasement. 'You could always call a taxi.'

'I'm damned if I will!' He gave her a hard look. 'Has it occurred to you that it might be *you* he's looking to for a little financial help along the way?'

She looked back at him in startled query. 'Why on earth would you think that? He never even met me before yesterday!'

'You think that would worry him? He's as capable of recognising a soft touch as the next opportunist.'

Rachel stiffened. 'Thanks!'

'It wasn't meant as an insult.' His tone was muted a little. 'You'd find it difficult to refuse him if he put out the begging-bowl.'

'Whereas you wouldn't, of course.' She was still smarting, and not about to forgo retaliation. 'You'd see him go down first, wouldn't you?'

The strong mouth twisted. 'If he were that close to penury he'd hardly be driving a Porsche still. With Gary it's all relative—always has been. He considers himself entitled to a part in all this, and won't much care how he gets it. The sooner you see through that surface charm of his the better!'

'I'll reserve judgement until I have some proof of his intentions,' Rachel returned stubbornly. 'He had a point with that Cain and Abel crack. You really hate him, don't you?'

'You've got it the wrong way round. Still——' with a shrug '—far be it from me to influence your opinions.'

They were in the library. Rachel bit her lip as he got up from the sofa where he had thrown himself in disgust just a few minutes before. She didn't want to leave things like this.

'I realise I hardly know him,' she said on a rational note, 'but, if it comes to that, I don't know you all that well either.' She registered the flick of an eyebrow with rancour, and tagged on sharply, 'That hardly counts!'

The sardonic tone increased. 'I was under the impression we were talking in biblical terms. We'll be getting to know each other a whole lot better in both contexts over the next few weeks. You wouldn't want to jeopardise that development, would you?'

It was Rachel's turn to effect a shrug, although everything in her cried out against the pretence. 'I can't see how Gary's being here is going to make any difference—especially as it will only be for a few days.'

'Given encouragement, he'll be here for as long as it takes,' came the hard reply. 'I can't force you to see things my way, but I can and will make life pretty uncomfortable for him if he does stay on. That's a promise!'

'Why?' she burst out. 'What did he do to make you so unforgiving towards him?'

'That,' he said, 'is between the two of us.'

'But he looks up to you,' Rachel insisted. 'He really admires you for escaping the way you did.'

Craig's laugh was short. 'He might approve the action. I've been bottom of his Christmas list for too many years to leave out the pinch of salt.' He made a resigned gesture. 'I'll fetch the car tomorrow instead.'

'If I'd been able to drive, none of this would have mattered,' Rachel murmured, and saw his lips slant afresh.

'It might have made things easier, true, but still wouldn't have excused Gary.' He studied her for a brief moment, his expression undergoing an indecipherable alteration. 'I fancy a swim,' he announced unexpectedly. 'In the sea, for preference. Are you game?'

'It will be cold,' Rachel warned. 'I mean *really* cold!'

'Only at first. The sun's warm enough.' There was a challenge in the grey gaze. 'Good for the circulation, anyway.'

'All right.' The agreement was out before she could think about it, and, having said it, she wasn't about to withdraw. In any case, it would be better if Craig was out of the way when Gary finally returned. 'Five minutes?'

'Make it ten,' he said. 'I'll need to phone the garage and let them know the change of plan. I don't want the Jag left out on the forecourt all night.'

Rachel left him to it, and went upstairs. Even with the sun shining so brightly, the thought of diving into the sea this early in the year sent a shiver down her back. Too late now to start having second thoughts, she told herself ruefully. If Craig could do it, she could do no less.

She donned a one-piece strapless costume in black and turquoise, and pulled on a tracksuit over the top. With a rolled towel under her arm, she went out to find Craig just emerging from his room. He too was wearing a tracksuit and was carrying a towel. He viewed her with an expression she found difficult to assess.

'Great minds think alike,' he observed. 'You look very sporty!'

'I feel very reluctant,' she admitted. 'I don't know how I allowed myself to be talked into this!'

'All down to the Lindhurst silver tongue.' Craig indicated the way ahead. 'Let's go.'

It was still only a little after three when they reached the beach. At least the water was calm, Rachel was thankful to see. She slid out of the tracksuit with a certain diffidence, very much aware of Craig's emerging semi-nudity. She had already taken up her hair in a swinging pony-tail. Seizing the initiative, she ran down to the water's edge and splashed through the shallows to plunge straight in before the chill could take hold.

It was cold certainly, but not to the degree she had anticipated. Or perhaps it was that her blood was already heated, she thought, striking out in a crawl scheduled to put rapid distance between her and the man she had left behind on the beach.

She had gone some considerable distance before he began to overhaul her; she could see him out of the corner of her eye when she turned her head to take in air, his powering arms flashing brilliant droplets as they scythed through the gentle waves. Short of practice herself, she was beginning to feel the strain already. Too much effort too quickly, she judged. She would have to turn back soon, like it or not.

The sudden cramping of muscle in her upper thigh took her totally by surprise; she floundered, went under, and came up spitting salt-water and panicking as the spasms tied her muscles into agonising knots.

Hands fastened under her armpits, dragging her on to her back. 'Massage it,' said Craig in her ear on a note so lacking in alarm that it calmed her immediately. She obeyed the injunction, and felt the pain ebbing at last. Craig was still holding her, supporting her head against his chest as he trod water. She fought the urge to turn and cling to him.

'OK now?' he asked.

'Yes, thanks.' Her voice sounded shaky to her ears. 'I'll be fine.'

'Just take it easy,' he advised. 'We're some way out.'

Something of an understatement, was Rachel's first thought on seeing just how far distant the shore was. Gingerly treading water, she pushed the wet hair from her face with a hand that felt like lead. It had been stupid of her to race out that way; she didn't need anyone to tell her that. If she had been alone, it might well have been her last swim.

'All you had to do was float on your back and massage the limb,' said Craig without censure. He was watching her face assessingly. 'Can you cope, or shall I tow you back?'

Rachel shook her head, too well aware of the effort that would entail over the distance involved. Craig was strong but he was also human.

'I'll manage,' she said. 'The pain's gone now.'

That it could also return, she knew, but there was no point in dwelling on the possibility. With Craig there to help, she'd get back all right. It was just going to take time.

It took even longer than she had allowed for, mostly because Craig insisted on her resting every few minutes. Her limbs felt rubbery when she at last staggered out on to firm sand. She sank down to sit with her head drooped over bent knees while she recovered her breath.

Craig sat down beside her. He was breathing faster than normal himself, but was not distressed. Rachel could see the fine hair on his thighs still sleeked with water. She couldn't restrain herself from putting out her hand to run a fingertip down one taut rope of muscle.

He said something short and sharp under his breath, then rolled to take hold of her, pushing her back into the sand as he kissed her with a passion that evoked instant response. Rachel clung to him the way she had wanted to do so badly out there, pressing herself against him in wanton disregard of anything and everything but the need of the moment, murmuring frantic little pleas she was scarcely aware of. She loved this man, and she wanted him, and there was nothing in the world that was going to keep them apart!

He peeled the swimsuit from her in one smooth motion, tossing it aside to devour her with his eyes while he divested himself of his trunks with equal dexterity. The tide was coming in, Rachel realised hazily, feeling the run of a wavelet up under her feet and calves, only it didn't seem to matter right now. She ran eager hands over him as he reared above her, guiding him to her, thrilling to the glorious sense of possession and of being possessed as they slid together in that merger of mergers—a fusing of mind and matter, of body and soul, of heaven and earth. The next wave rolled right under them, but went unheeded as the wildness swept her away. There never had been, never could be, a moment greater than this, was her last thought before the sky fell in on her.

Sense and sanity returned slowly but inexorably. The realisation that it was still broad daylight and far from the privacy and security of the bedroom jerked Rachel into sudden appalled movement. It was only the swiftness of Craig's own reaction that kept her from scrambling to her feet in panic at the thought of being overlooked.

'Too late,' he murmured, holding her easily as she struggled against him. 'There's no one else here but the two of us—unless you count a few gulls.' He dropped a light kiss on her mouth when she subsided again, supporting his weight on his forearms as he looked down at her with the flame still smouldering in his eyes. 'You're like two different people rolled into one! Just lie still, will you, and give the inhibitions a rest? You can't come on to a man the way you just did and expect to simply walk away the moment it's over.'

'I wasn't planning on walking,' Rachel managed on a husky note. 'Running, perhaps.'

'Why?' he queried softly. 'You don't exactly hate what we do together.'

'It's not so much the "what" at the moment,' she acknowledged with an attempt at humour, 'it's the place and time. I . . . forgot where we were.'

A smile touched his lips. 'Flattering!'

'It wasn't meant that way,' she denied. The water-line was under her waist now, her lower legs almost completely submerged. She added pleadingly, 'If you don't let me up we'll be swimming again soon! I'm covered in sand, and it isn't very comfortable.'

'I'm coming to the same conclusion,' he agreed. 'A pity, but there you are. I'd suggest we go back in for a rinse before we dry ourselves off.'

Rachel sat up as he moved away from her. It was quite ridiculous, she knew, to feel in any way self-conscious after what had just taken place between them, but she still found it difficult to rise to her feet and accompany him into the sea with any degree of aplomb.

She found it even more so when he took it upon himself to rid her of the clinging sand by scooping handfuls of water over her shoulders and breasts. She went right under in order to stop him, swimming away from him to surface a few feet away and scramble for the comparative safety of the shore. Laughing, he followed her out, seizing a towel and wrapping it about her, then rubbing vigorously until she yelled in protest.

'That'll teach you,' he said, though quite what it was supposed to teach her Rachel wasn't at all sure.

Dried and dressed again—though both minus the underwear they had forgotten to bring—they rinsed out their soiled swimwear and wrapped them in the damp towels. The afternoon was almost gone, the sun no longer hot. Gary would most probably be back by the time they reached the house, Rachel thought, and knew a swift reluctance to be involved in the ruckus that was sure to come when Craig laid eyes on him.

'Do you think we could forget the car business and spend a pleasant evening?' she ventured on the way. 'I know Gary shouldn't have taken the Rolls like that, but——'

'But it happened, and going on about it isn't going to change anything,' Craig broke in shortly. 'That is what you were going to say, isn't it?'

'Something like that,' she acknowledged. 'He'll be gone in a few days. I'd just like things to stay reasonably peaceful while he is here, that's all. It's not so much to ask, is it?'

Tall, lean and overpoweringly masculine in the black tracksuit, Craig inclined his head. 'Maybe not from my side. I can't vouch for Gary. All right, so we forget about the car. How about that candle-lit dinner for two tonight?' He glanced her way when she failed to answer immediately, expression hardening. 'Don't even consider letting my brother make a difference. He can either go out himself, or eat on his own.'

She had won one concession; it was too much to hope for another, Rachel reflected. In any case, she didn't want to say no. Gary must make his own choice.

'All right, tonight,' she agreed, and was rewarded with a brief but reassuring smile.

'That's more like it.'

More like what? she wondered—the kind of pliant, submissive wife he would prefer? If so, he was out of luck. Love him she might, kowtow to him she would not!

Without checking the courtyard, there was no telling whether or not the Rolls had returned. Certainly, there was no sign of Gary when they got indoors. In a house this size he could be anywhere, of course, Rachel reflected on parting from Craig to shower and dress. There were no 'no go' areas.

Standing under the warm running water, she allowed her thoughts to dwell luxuriantly on the events of the past hour. Making love with Craig was an experience to end all experiences; she could never in a million years grow tired of it—or of him either, for that matter. Only how long would it be before he grew bored with *her*?

Could one woman ever be enough for a man accustomed to freedom of choice? Without mutual love to hold them together, there seemed little chance of a long and happy marriage.

Unless a child changed things. She ran experimental fingers down over her smooth abdomen, smiling wryly at her own flight of fancy. It was a hope to cling to.

She found both brothers in the library when she went down. Judging from Gary's cheerful greeting, Craig had kept his word about the Rolls. He was certainly congenial enough on the surface.

'I hear you're going out tonight,' said the younger man without appearing in the least put out. 'Dare I suspect romance in the air?'

'You can suspect anything you like,' responded his brother levelly. 'Do you plan on eating here?'

Just for a moment there was a spark in the hazel eyes. 'Where else?'

'I already told Mrs Brantley you would be,' put in Rachel hastily. She felt bound to add, 'I hope you won't find it too lonely.'

Gary smiled and shrugged. 'I can always appeal to Doreen for company if I get desperate.'

'She leaves at six,' said Craig, still without change of inflexion. 'And she has a regular boyfriend.'

'What you really mean is "no dallying with the staff".' Gary's tone was light, but the edge wasn't far off. 'Disappointing. She's a little cracker! Still, I always abide by the rules of the house. When do you plan on starting work on this book, did you say?'

'Tomorrow.' Craig glanced in Rachel's direction. 'I'll need your help to get the ideas down on paper. You may even be able to suggest names for a couple of characters I'm stuck on.'

She sparkled, Gary forgotten for the moment. 'I'd love to try!'

'I'd hold out for a percentage of the royalties too,' advised the other man. He sounded just a little caustic. 'Not that either of you are going to be needing the money.'

'What would you propose?' asked Craig with deceptive calm. 'Making the rights over to you, maybe?'

The satire drew no more than a short laugh. 'I certainly wouldn't throw the offer in your face!'

'I'm sure.' Craig gave him back look for look. 'Unfortunately, it's one I'm likely to be making.'

'Here's tea,' Rachel interposed with relief at the rattle of the trolley outside the door. 'It's a bit late for it, I know, but I was thirsty.'

Whatever reply Gary had been about to make to the flat statement he kept it to himself, although the enmity in his eyes was plain for all to see. Craig had been right, Rachel thought; the hatred was all Gary's. Just why he should feel such bitterness was a question yet to be answered.

He was still upstairs in his room when they left the house at seven-thirty. As usual, Craig was doing the driving. Something would have to be done eventually with both Grayson and the Rolls, Rachel acknowledged. She couldn't see herself holding out for long against Craig's insistence that she should learn to drive. It would make life easier, she had to admit.

They went inland to a restaurant near Chillerton, to which Craig had been recommended by no less a personage than Mrs Brantley herself. An excellent endorsement, they agreed after a meal to satisfy the most exacting of tastes. Small and old and intimately lit, the ambience of the place was pleasing too.

'Did you mean it about starting work tomorrow?' Rachel asked over coffee.

'Any reason why I shouldn't have meant it?' countered Craig on a note that brought her eyes up to his face, bronzed even deeper by the flickering candle-light.

'Well, no. Just that you seemed to be saying it more for Gary's benefit than because you were in any real tearing hurry to make a start.'

'You keep bringing his name up,' came the taut comment. 'Feeling sorry for him, by any chance?'

'A certain sympathy, I suppose,' she admitted, refusing to lie about it. 'If I knew the reason why he feels the way he obviously does about you, it might help me to appreciate your views.'

'My version is bound to be one-sided,' Craig pointed out after a moment's silence. 'Gary sees things differently.' He paused again, studying her features as if in some doubt still of revealing too much. 'It started when he was in his mid-teens,' he said at length. 'I discovered he was into drugs—not just using them himself, but persuading others to get involved too. To cut a long story short, I gave him an ultimatum. Either he voluntarily entered a clinic to be dried out, and guaranteed to stay clean, or I'd turn him in to the authorities as a pusher. He chose the clinic.'

'But never forgave you for it.' Rachel looked back at him steadily. 'Would you have done—turned him in, I mean?'

'Yes.' The tone was unequivocal. 'Ruining his own health was one thing, dragging in other kids something else again. I kept a pretty close eye on him after he came out. If he'd stepped out of line just once I'd have followed through, and he knew it. It didn't endear me to him.'

'I imagine not.' Rachel reached across impulsively to lay her hand over his where it rested on the table between them. 'You did the right thing, Craig. He had to be stopped. He might have been dead by now if you hadn't done what you did.'

'Or worse,' he agreed. 'Not that you'd ever get Gary to see it like that. He's no idiot, by any means, but, like a lot of others, he wants everything handed to him on a platter. For a couple of years or so he seemed to be making good, then the bottom fell out of it all and he was back to square one, or near enough. Whatever I offered him, it wouldn't be nearly as much as he considers himself due, and I'm not prepared to enter into any kind of long-term commitment. I wouldn't see him totally down and out, but that's as far as it goes. If that comes across as hard, well, too bad.'

'It's understandable,' Rachel responded hesitantly, and saw the grey eyes take on a certain cynicism.

'But?'

She lifted her shoulders in wry acknowledgement. 'I was just thinking that it might be easier all round to make over a sum sufficient to set him up in some kind of business on the proviso that he doesn't keep coming back for more.'

'It wouldn't work. He'd see it as a sign of weakness, nothing else. As I said earlier, if he's so hard up he can sell the Porsche for starters. It's worth around twenty thousand at market value. Then there's the flat.'

'But then he'd have nowhere to live.'

'So he'd have to find somewhere cheaper.' If there had been tolerance in his voice at all, it was gone now. 'Whatever happens, I don't want you involved, is that clear?'

'Oh, perfectly!' She snatched back her hand, bristling herself now. 'One thing you seem to have forgotten, Craig, is that I inherited the right to do anything I choose with my share. If I wanted to give the lot away, I don't need your permission!'

'True.' The lean features were austere. 'So I'm *asking* you not to get involved. Does that salve your pride?'

The anger faded as swiftly as it had arisen, leaving Rachel depressedly aware of having put a damper on the whole evening. And for what?

'That was silly of me,' she proffered. 'Of course I shan't get involved. He's *your* brother.'

There was no immediate easing of tension. Craig continued to regard her with that same cold appraisement for several seconds before finally inclining his head in a dismissive gesture.

'Let's forget it,' he said. 'Have some more coffee.'

They managed to achieve some semblance of the easy camaraderie they had enjoyed earlier, but it wasn't for real, Rachel knew. Such spats might well become commonplace when they were married, because neither of them was accustomed to making concessions. With Charles there had never been any reason for disagreement. Their life together had been harmonious to a degree.

Oddly enough, she felt no sense of nostalgia for that harmony. Craig might lack the tolerant understanding and gentlemanly attitude of his uncle, but he had introduced her to heights she might never have known without him. Love came in many guises; she was only just beginning the appreciate that fact. Her feelings for Charles had been on another plane altogether.

Driving back to Apperknowle through the dark and narrow country lanes, she wondered if Craig would expect to spend the night together. After this afternoon, it was hardly feasible to keep on protesting. She wanted to be with him. Every fibre in her thrilled to the thought. She was sorry now that she had been so adamantly against the immediate ceremony he had first suggested. It didn't matter when, only what they made of it afterwards.

They would tie the knot as soon as the three weeks were up, she decided there and then. Others could accept it or not, as they chose. Her mother would have other things on her mind, anyway.

Gary was still up, and looking less than contented with his lot. He'd spent the evening watching television, he said, for what it was worth. Rachel tried to turn a deaf ear, but found it difficult to be entirely unsympathetic to his cause. He was, after all, a Lindhurst by birth, which was more than she was herself.

Perhaps recognising the symptoms, Craig made no effort to join her for the night. He took his leave of her at her bedroom door with a kiss that left a whole lot to be desired. Sulking wasn't the word to describe his attitude, she thought unhappily. Deliberated restraint was closer. If he was out to teach her that crossing him didn't pay, he was succeeding. Only it wasn't going to make her any more amenable either.

CHAPTER TEN

TRUE to his word, Craig indicated that he was ready to begin work on his synopsis right after breakfast. Gary, he said, would no doubt find entertainment of some kind.

With the study door closed against human intrusion, and the windows opened on fresh sweet air, he seemed in no great rush to get down to it, tapping a pencil lightly on the desk-edge as he sat contemplating the far wall.

Rachel waited without speaking. The desk she had used herself when Charles was alive was set at right angles, with an expensive electric typewriter in central position. Charles hadn't held with word processors, much to her relief. This particular machine was capable of making alterations with the minimum of fuss and no visible evidence, which was all that was really needed. She flexed her fingers in readiness for the flow of ideas to be drafted into notes from which the synopsis of the novel would be formulated.

The ringing of the telephone brought instinctive and immediate action. She had the receiver in her hand before Craig had moved a muscle. 'Apperknowle?'

'Oh, Rachel,' said her mother, 'I'm just ringing to remind you about the craft fair on Saturday. You will be coming, I hope?'

'Of course.' She *had* forgotten, but wasn't about to admit it. 'I always do. What time?'

'The usual—nine o'clockish for a ten o'clock opening. I'll be setting out the stall the night before, so it will just

be a case of helping out with the ticketing and selling.'
Laura paused. 'Do you think Craig might want to lend
a hand? It gets quite hectic, as you know.'

'I've no idea,' Rachel replied, conscious of the subject
under discussion's eyes on her. 'Hang on a minute.' She
covered the mouthpiece with her hand. 'Mom wants to
know if you'd be interested in helping out at the craft
fair on Saturday? You don't have to feel obligated.'

Dark brows lifted. 'I'm sure. Tell her yes, I'd be happy
to.'

She hesitated before saying cautiously, 'What about
Gary?'

'What about him? Hopefully, he'll be gone by then.'

'But if he isn't?'

Impatience clouded his expression. 'I'm not his keeper.
He's capable of looking after himself.'

Resignedly, she took her hand from the mouthpiece.
'He says he'd be delighted.'

'Oh, how nice of him!' Laura was obviously delighted
too. 'It's time he started meeting people.'

Rachel hadn't thought of it that way, but her mother
was right; it had to happen some time. Perhaps when
people realised what kind of man Craig was, they would
make more allowances for the speed with which the two
of them had apparently become close.

And pigs might fly, come the cynical rider.

'I'll have to go now, Mom,' she said. 'We're supposed
to be working.'

'On the book? Oh, lord, you should have told me!
Apologise to Craig for me, will you?'

Replacing the receiver, Rachel passed on the message,
hardly surprised when he shrugged it off.

'We were hardly what you'd call going strong. To tell
you the truth, I'm finding difficulty in getting started at

all.' Smile rueful, he tapped his forehead. 'It's all in here, but dictating it is the problem.'

'So why don't you write everything out in longhand on your own, and let me type it up later?' she suggested. 'My sitting here waiting like this must be very off-putting.'

He looked at her for a moment without answering, an unreadable expression in his eyes. 'What will you do with yourself meanwhile?'

'What I've done for the last six months, I suppose,' she said. 'Not a lot. I can take another few days of it without running amok with frustration.'

'With Gary for company?'

Rachel stiffened, sentient to the nuances in the observation. 'Do I take that the way it sounds?'

'That would depend,' he said, 'on how you thought it sounded.'

'As if you didn't trust me to be alone with him for any length of time,' she flashed. 'As if the two of us were going to gang up against you the moment your back was turned! You said yesterday that you weren't paranoid about him, but I think you are. You can't allow him one redeeming feature, can you?'

The skin around the firm mouth had paled from the pressure brought to bear. He made no move, just sat there looking at her in narrowed reflection. 'Oh, I can. He's a regular charmer when he needs to be. And you're the ideal target. He already has you softened up for the kill. I meant what I said last night, Rachel. I don't want you involving yourself in my family problems. Your hands are tied, anyway, until we fulfil the terms of the will.'

'In which case, you don't have anything to worry about, do you?' She was gathering herself as she spoke, too incensed by his attitude to stay and listen to any more. 'I'll make my own mind up about your brother, thank you. So far as I'm concerned, he's here as a guest and I'll treat him that way!'

She took care to close the door quietly on her way out, instead of slamming it the way every instinct in her prompted her to do. No way would she allow him to know how deeply he had hurt her. For her to offer Gary money would be tantamount to kicking him in the face. She might have intimated such action in temper last night, but she had also retracted in no mean terms. Obviously her word meant little.

She hadn't intended going looking for Gary, but neither did she intend avoiding him. Coming across him in the drawing-room, where he was perusing the morning newspapers in desultory fashion, she closed her mind to Craig's warnings and treated the younger man to a warm smile.

'How would you feel about running me to Newport?' she asked on impulse. 'It would save taking the Rolls.'

'It would save me from utter boredom too,' he confessed, returning the smile. 'I thought you and Craig were working all morning?'

'Writer's block,' she said glibly. 'I left him to it. If you're not against walking round a few shops with me first, we could have lunch in town. I know a very good little place.'

The surprise was swiftly cancelled, replaced by gratified approval. 'I could never say no to a beautiful woman! Let's go.'

Rachel laughed, holding up a staying hand. 'Give me a few minutes to change.'

'Don't,' he said. 'You're perfect as you are.'

'A regular charmer when he needs to be' came the words in her inner ear, but she resolutely shut them out. 'And you're a born flatterer,' she told him lightly. 'I'll see you outside in ten minutes.'

She found time, while she changed her trousers and shirt for a lightweight wool suit in beige and cream, to question the wisdom of deliberately flouting Craig this way, but what he had said still rankled too much to make her consider withdrawing the invitation. Gary would be her brother-in-law when she married Craig; that surely meant something. It harmed nothing and no one at least to be friendly towards him.

He had brought the Porsche round to the front when she went down. Her freedom to choose notwith-standing, she was glad that the study was on the far side of the house. Craig would only discover their absence when he emerged for lunch. The fact that she would have to face his no doubt scathing critique when they re-turned was neither here nor there at the moment. She was doing, and would continue to do, her own thing.

Gary drove the sports car far too fast for her taste. He was flamboyant in everything he did, she realised—like a little boy showing off, in many ways. His rakish good looks and ready wit brought assistants flocking in all the shops they visited. He even picked out a couple of dresses he declared were just her, and insisted she try them on.

Shorter by inches than she was accustomed to wearing, and daring in style, they certainly made her look dif-ferent, Rachel had to admit, but she wasn't sure if it was a difference she really liked. It was only to satisfy him that she finally bought one of them, along with the knee-high red leather boots that went with it.

'Fashion accessories,' he said when she laughingly protested the need for such items with summer coming on. 'Nothing to do with the weather. You should come up to town some time to see the fashion scene at its best.' He added easily, 'In fact, why not soon? I could squire you around. I'd like that. We could have a really good time together.'

In what context? Rachel wondered. She shook her head, but kept the smile going. 'A nice idea, but I'm afraid I'll be tied up.'

They were in the restaurant she had chosen, and almost finished with the meal. Gary gave her a thoughtful look.

'Tied up with what?'

'Oh...' lifting her shoulders '...just things.'

But Gary wasn't about to leave it at that. 'Such as? You were only telling me a few minutes ago how empty your life had been since Charles died.'

Rachel bit her lip, aware of having talked herself into a corner. In a way, she supposed she had been preparing him for the news that she was to marry his brother, although she hadn't intended to impart it in full as yet. On the other hand, when *would* the time be right?

'There's something you should know,' she said. 'Only you have to promise to keep it to yourself.'

He made an exaggerated gesture, crossing his heart. 'On my honour!'

She wasn't quite sure how to say it. In the end there was only one way, and that was straight out. 'Charles decreed that Craig and I have to marry in order to inherit the estate. He wanted the name to be carried on.'

Gary looked totally blank. 'You mean,' he said slowly, 'that you neither of you gets anything if you don't comply?'

'Craig doesn't. I'm financially secure whatever happens. The main thing is, Apperknowle would go under the hammer.'

'And you'd marry him just to keep a house?'

She flushed. 'It isn't just a house, it's a piece of history! I don't want to see it turned into a holiday centre!'

'There's worse things.' His face revealed a conflict of emotions. 'As you said, you don't suffer financially whatever.'

'There's more to life than money,' she retorted. 'In any case, I'd be robbing your brother of his inheritance.'

'And, being the kind of person you are, you can't bring yourself to do that.' Gary studied her in some bemusement. 'I don't think I ever met anyone quite that magnanimous before!'

The flush deepened. Telling him how she felt about Craig, when the latter himself didn't know, was obviously out of the question. It was a secret that would remain locked in her heart, unless there ever came a time when those feelings were returned.

'It's the only answer,' she said. 'I promised Charles.'

'He actually mentioned Craig by name?'

'Yes.' She knew what he was getting at, but chose to ignore it. 'Apparently he saw him as the right man to carry on the line.'

'Well, bully for Craig!' The bitterness was undisguised. 'I hope you realise what kind of life you'll have with *him* for a husband? He never heard of equality—in any sphere! Look how he's already roped you in to help with this book he's supposed to be writing. Why can't he bring someone in from outside?' He gave her no time to form a reply. 'I'll tell you why! Because he's too damned tight to pay anyone. Always has been, always will be, no matter how much he has!'

His voice had risen, drawing curious glances from nearby tables. Rachel put down her spoon with fingers that felt suddenly stiff. 'I think I'd like to get back.'

Gary got a hold on himself with obvious effort. He even managed to look shamefaced. 'Sorry about that. It's been building up a long time. You don't know the half of what I've put up with over the years!'

'It isn't really my business,' she said uncomfortably. 'I'm sorry too, Gary, but I can't start taking sides.' She made a pretence of glancing at her watch. 'And it really is time we got back. I never meant to be out this long.'

His mouth was a thin straight line. 'You see? He's got you jumping through hoops already. You'd do better to forget about promises and go for what's yours!'

If she hadn't been head over heels in love with Craig, she might well have agreed with him, Rachel thought hollowly. Good for her or not, however, she couldn't give him up.

The drive back to Apperknowle was accomplished at a speed and with a lack of care that had her heart in her mouth more than once. She tried remonstrating, but received no response. From the set of Gary's jaw, and general air of hostility, she gathered that friendly relations had been withdrawn. There was little enough she could do about it. Only Craig himself could make the move to straighten things out, and he was adamant.

He wasn't in evidence when they reached the house. When asked, Mrs Brantley advised that he had asked for lunch to be brought to the study, and, so far as she knew, he was in there still. Which meant there was a faint chance, Rachel thought, that he wouldn't know she had been out. She regretted asking Gary to go with her in the first place, and even more so telling him about the terms of the will. Craig would be furious if he found out, although, as he'd been the one to let his mother in on the act, he had little room to complain.

Gary had disappeared. To where, she neither knew nor very much cared at the moment. She went to get out of the beige suit and into something a little more casual, briefly considered popping into the study to see how it was going, then rejected the idea on the grounds that he would hardly welcome any interruption.

With more than an hour to go before tea, she tried to settle down to finish the novel she hadn't opened since Craig's return from London, but the words failed to grip her. Eventually, she gave it up and went through to the drawing-room to open up the grand piano. She wasn't a brilliant pianist, but Charles had always liked to hear her play. She began now with one of his favourites—the waltz from *Sleeping Beauty*.

It must have been ten or even fifteen minutes later that she looked up to see Craig standing in the doorway. He was still wearing the same grey trousers and shirt he had had on that morning, she noted as her fingers faltered on the keys and came to a halt.

'I'm sorry,' she said. 'Did I disturb you?'

He shook his head. 'I was enjoying it. I didn't realise you played.'

'I'm badly out of practice,' she deprecated. 'It's the first time since Charles——' She broke off, a wry little smile touching her lips. 'Quite some time, anyway. Do you play yourself?'

'No,' he admitted. He had come over to the piano, and was standing with an elbow resting lightly on the frame, face relaxed. 'I never got round to learning an instrument, more's the pity. You never realise what you're missing until it's too late.'

'You could always start now,' she said.

He laughed. 'I don't see myself struggling with scales at my age. I'm happy enough to sit back and listen. Do carry on.'

'I think I've had enough for the time being.' Rachel closed down the lid again with care, and added steadily, 'How did it go?'

'Not bad.' His tone was casual. 'You were right about writing things down in longhand. I'll be ready to start the synopsis proper tomorrow. Sorry about sticking with it through lunch. I found it difficult to stop once I got started.'

From the sound of it, he was unaware of her desertion—a state of affairs unlikely to last long once Gary put in an appearance, she realised. She was about to tell him when the latter walked into the room.

'I thought I heard music,' he remarked. 'Recital over, is it?'

'For today,' Rachel confirmed. There was no way of conveying to him her wish to have their excursion kept a secret; nor, from the look still in his eyes, would he have responded to it if there were. Both Craig and herself were probably right off his Christmas list now.

'Did you see the dress we bought this morning?' Gary asked Craig with smiling deliberation. 'More of a wide belt, I suppose you could call it, but, with legs like Rachel's, why hide them?'

The pause seemed to stretch forever. Rachel forced herself to meet the steely gaze. 'Gary drove me into Newport to do some shopping, as you didn't need me,' she said, and knew her voice gave her away. 'I thought

Mrs Brantley would have told you when she brought in your lunch.'

'She didn't.' The words were clipped. 'I didn't realise you were into minis!'

I'm not, was what she wanted to say, but trying to explain her reasons for buying the dress, when she hardly understood them herself, was out of the question. 'I fancied a change,' she said instead. 'I've been stuck in a rut fashion-wise for far too long.' She got up jerkily from the piano-stool, cross with herself for feeling guilt where none was due. 'It must be almost teatime.'

'It's only half-past three,' Gary supplied. His expression was bland. 'I think I might go for a swim. Double congratulations, by the way, Craig. I hear there's a wedding in the offing.'

There was silence in the room after he had gone. Craig was the first to break it. 'I was under the impression,' he said tautly, 'that you didn't want anyone else to know.'

'You told your mother,' Rachel returned on a defensive note.

'But you haven't told yours yet. Don't you think her entitlement is greater than my brother's?'

She spread her hands in a helpless gesture. 'It just...came out.'

'Oh, sure! The kind of thing that just slips into a conversation by accident!'

'Well, it did!' She sought refuge in an anger of her own. 'What difference does it make, in any case? We both know the reason we're marrying at all is to get what each of us wants. The rest is incidental.'

'Is it?' There was a dangerous spark in his eyes. 'Let's see just *how* incidental!'

Hemmed in by the heavy stool at her rear, she had no chance to avoid him as he reached for her. Dragging her from the piano, he swung her up into his arms to carry her over to the nearest sofa and drop her on to the cushions. Rachel struggled wildly as he pinned her down with both hands on her shoulders, but it was like fighting a tank. His mouth on hers was ruthless in its demanding, unremitting pressure, his tongue a lever forcing her lips to part and let him in, penetrating her defences with its scorching exploration.

And somehow she was answering that demand with one of her own, not even caring where they were, only aware of the tumultuous pounding in her ears, of the rage in her heart and the urgency of her need.

Her blouse was open to the waist, his hand at her breast. She gasped at the urgency of his caresses, yet she didn't want it to stop. The anger in him was a spur to emotions hitherto untapped. She wanted to be taken forcefully, by sheer brute strength—to be subdued by this man she loved to hate. When he pulled back it was like a slap in the face. She could only lie there looking at him with eyes as dark as night.

'So tell me now that it doesn't mean anything to you,' he invited harshly. 'Tell me you don't like what I do to you!'

'Craig.' His name came out low and husky. 'Don't be this way.'

There was no melting of the ice in his eyes. 'Which way would you expect me to be? You made a statement, I just refuted it. If we have nothing else, we have this!'

Rachel winced as his thumb roughly stroked over her hardened nipple, not in pain so much as an aching sense of loss. Yet how could she lose what she had never had? He hadn't at any time made out that his feelings for her ran any deeper.

'It isn't going to be enough,' she whispered.

'It's sufficient for the purpose,' he returned hardly. 'Maybe already has been. We'll go through with it regardless. As you said, that way we both get what we want. The rest we can call a bonus. Imagine what it might have been like if you'd found me physically repulsive? Come to think of it, what *would* you have done in those circumstances?'

'A promise is a promise,' Rachel forced out through stiff lips. 'I'd have kept my word to Charles in the end, come what may.'

'A point of honour?' Craig's tone seared. 'The sacrifice to end all sacrifices! He really cared about you, didn't he?'

'Yes, he did!' She was in no position to beg further retaliation, but neither was she about to allow him to get away with the slur on the man she had loved so dearly if so differently. 'He cared in a way you couldn't even begin to appreciate—and he trusted me to keep faith. *I* loved *him* the way I'll never love any other man!'

The skin looked stretched over the hard male cheekbones, all expression wiped away. 'Just so long as we both know where we stand.'

Rachel remained where she was as he rose abruptly to his feet. She felt frozen inside. I didn't mean it, she wanted to say; but what was the use? She had already said far too much.

CHAPTER ELEVEN

THE day passed somehow. Craig didn't put in an appearance at dinner. He had said he was going out, Mrs Brantley advised when asked, obviously taken aback that Rachel wasn't aware of it.

'Secrets already?' suggested Gary with surprisingly little malice. 'Hardly a good foundation.'

'We're not married yet,' Rachel pointed out, determined not to let him see her upset by the desertion. 'Even when we are, we'll still be individuals, perfectly entitled to do what we feel like doing.' She added levelly, 'Talking of secrets, I asked you to keep what I told you to yourself.'

'I didn't realise it applied to Craig too,' he said on a note of apology she found disconcerting. 'I guess he was none too pleased over your letting me in on the act?'

'No, he wasn't.' She toyed with her soup-spoon, uncertain how to take this change in attitude. 'It's a very awkward situation.' And was *that* the understatement of the year! she thought depressedly.

A moment or two passed before Gary made any further contribution. 'There could,' he observed, 'be an alternative to marrying Craig.'

'There is,' she agreed. 'I already told you, it means breaking my word to Charles.'

'You might not have to do that either.'

Rachel stared at him. 'I don't think I understand.'

'It's simple enough. I telephoned a lawyer friend of mine earlier, and put the whole thing to him. He thinks

171

there may be a chance that a court would rule it's only the actual Lindhurst name that's the essential requirement. Well, I'm a Lindhurst too.'

He couldn't be serious, Rachel thought dazedly. It had to be his idea of a joke! Only it wasn't; she could see that from his expression. He meant every word.

'I don't know where you got the impression that I was looking for a way out of marrying your brother,' she managed with reasonable calm, 'but you're quite wrong. He's Charles's choice.'

'All Charles wanted was for the name to be carried on,' Gary argued. 'I'm as capable as Craig is of fathering a son and heir—and I'd be willing to let you have complete charge.' He was leaning forward across the table, eager, persuasive, wholly accustomed to getting his own way with the female sex. 'We make a good-looking couple. Life could be real fun together. I know you're attracted to me the same way I am to you. We both of us felt it the moment we clapped eyes on each other. It's why you didn't want me to leave, isn't it? *Isn't* it?' he insisted.

Rachel scarcely knew whether to laugh or cry; either of which reactions would be verging on hysteria. She took a grip on herself with every ounce of self-control she could conjure.

'The only reason I asked you to stay,' she said, 'was because I felt some sense of obligation. If I'd realised you were going to take it as some kind of avowal, I'd have let Craig have his way. I'm not in any way attracted to you as a man, Gary, so you can put that idea right out of your head. I want a husband I can respect and rely on.'

'And you think you'll get that with Craig?' The handsome features were handsome no longer. 'You really believe he's going to stick around this place once he's tied everything up?'

'Until he's finished this novel he's writing, yes,' she replied. 'After that, it's entirely up to him.'

'That Goody Two Shoes act of yours is just a veneer, isn't it?' he sneered. 'Underneath, you're just as calculating as he is!'

'If you want to see it that way.' Rachel was nearing the end of her tether. 'I think it might be a good thing if you left, Gary. The ferries are still running. You could be home by midnight at the pace you drive.'

'*You're* not throwing me out!' he retorted savagely. 'Charles was my uncle. I have a right to be here!'

Trembling, and trying not to show it, she said thickly, 'Perhaps you'd rather wait until Craig gets back and hears your proposition? I doubt if he'll find it amusing.'

For a lengthy moment he glared at her with venom in his eyes, then he threw down his napkin with an expletive that shook her. 'I'll go,' he gritted, 'but you haven't heard the last of this. I'm taking it to court, do you hear? I'll fight the two of you every inch of the way!'

Rachel sat in stunned and quivering silence as he stormed from the room. He didn't have a leg to stand on, that part of her mind still rational enough to reason at all told her; but then, she was no lawyer. Craig would have to be told, of course. This wasn't something she could possibly keep to herself. If he'd been here none of it would have happened.

Not tonight, perhaps, came the thought, but sooner or later Gary would have presented his ridiculous notion. He was everything Craig had said: interested only in furthering his own ends.

Mrs Brantley brought in the pot-roast. She looked surprised to see Rachel sitting there alone at the table.

'Will Mr Lindhurst be long, do you think?' she asked tactfully. 'I can always take his back to keep hot until he's ready.'

'He has to leave,' Rachel told her. 'Something cropped up that he has to deal with back home.'

There had been no telephone calls during the last couple of hours, which made nonsense of the excuse, but the housekeeper accepted it at face value. 'A shame he didn't have time to finish his meal,' she said, 'but I dare say he'll get something on the ferry.'

She served some of the meat on to a ready-warmed plate from the dinner-wagon, and brought it across to exchange it for the soup dish still containing a couple of inches of liquid. Vegetable tureens were placed on the table within easy reach, and the lids removed for Rachel to help herself from the contents.

With food the last thing on her mind, she took a spoonful from each dish and made a show of picking up her knife and fork. Only when Mrs Brantley had gone from the room did she lay them down again to sit gazing numbly at her plate, wondering if she couldn't have handled things better.

The sound of a car engine some minutes later brought her head upright. Not the Mercedes returning, she judged, but the Porsche leaving. Craig had forgotten to go and pick up the Jaguar, she thought irrelevantly. He must have been really immersed in his work! Where he was now, she couldn't begin to guess. All she did know was that she wanted him desperately to be here with her.

It was gone midnight when he finally put in an appearance. Rachel had waited in the library for the sound of the car. She went out to the hall on the opening of the outer door.

Wearing the mid-grey suit he had worn that very first evening, he looked every inch a man of stature and style. His expression as he glanced at her was remote.

'There was no need to wait up,' he said, closing and locking the door behind him. 'I'm as security-conscious as needs be.'

'Gary's gone,' she told him, unable to find any other way of broaching the subject. 'He left almost four hours ago.'

The dark brows came together. 'Why?'

'Because I told him to.' Rachel drew in a long and steadying breath. 'He has some crazy idea that he can take over from you as legatee if he challenges the will in court. He couldn't, could he?'

'Not unless he's come up with some way of proving that Charles was of unsound mind when he drafted it— and even then it would probably be you who'd benefit.' Craig sounded remarkably matter-of-fact about it. 'I gather you didn't fancy the idea yourself?'

'Of course I didn't!' She was stung by the intimation that she might have even considered it. 'I could no more——' She broke off, catching her lower lip between her teeth as his mouth took on a slant.

'He doesn't make you feel the way I make you feel?'

'No one makes me feel the way you make me feel.' She could say that with truth. She paused, searching his face for some sign of encouragement; then, finding none, but she continued anyway, 'Craig, about this morning...I didn't set out with the intention of telling Gary everything. I didn't even intend asking him to take me to Newport. It just...happened.'

'Because you were furious with me for laying down the law, and needed to show me where to get off.' His tone was unrelenting. 'That's about the sum of it, isn't it?'

Rachel nodded unhappily. 'It was stupid of me. You're right about Gary. He doesn't care about anyone or anything except number one. If I learned nothing else today, I learned that much.'

'That's something.' He looked at her as if waiting for more, lifting his shoulders in a brief shrug when she stayed silent. 'If that's it, I'm going to bed.'

'Can I come with you?' The words were out before she was conscious of forming the thought. She flushed hotly as he turned back to study her with a sardonically lifted brow, but stood her ground. 'If, as you said earlier, this is all we have, then hadn't we better make the most of it?'

For a moment she was afraid he was going to turn her down, then he shrugged again and inclined his head. 'Why not?'

Accompanying him up the stairs, she found time to wonder at her own temerity. The Rachel of a couple of weeks ago would never have dreamed of offering herself in such a manner.

Not even that much, in fact, she realised, counting backwards. Taking into account Craig's trip to London, they had spent just seven days in total together. Seven days, seven years—what difference did it make? She loved him. That was all she cared about.

Whatever he might be lacking in deeper emotion, his lovemaking left nothing to be desired. Time and time again he brought her to the brink, holding her there with a practised technique that had her moaning for release before finally and devastatingly claiming her for his own.

He was in charge, and letting her know it, and she revelled in the knowledge. Love her or not, she was his for all time.

Later, lying with her head on his chest and his arm heavy across her waist and hip, she said softly, 'Where *did* you go tonight, Craig?'

He made no reply for a moment, although he didn't appear to resent the question. When he did speak, it was levelly. 'I took your mother out to dinner.'

'Mom?' Rachel lifted her head to look at him, unable to read his expression in the darkness. 'Why?'

'I thought it was time she knew the truth.' The arm shifted upwards as she stiffened, holding her down. 'There's every chance that my mother will tell her, anyway, when she goes up to town next week. They want everything she's done, and more to come. She got the news this afternoon.'

'She might have phoned to tell me first.' The hurt of it was there in her voice.

'She didn't think you were all that interested.'

'That's not true!'

'Then it's up to you to convince her.'

'I will.' Rachel subsided again, stifling further protests. 'How did she take it? About...us, I mean?'

'Surprisingly well, considering.' There was an unexpected hint of humour. 'She said you could do a lot worse.'

'She thinks more of you than she thought of Charles, then.'

'I'm younger than Charles.' The humour had dissipated. 'Would you like more proof of that?'

'You don't have to prove anything,' Rachel assured him huskily. 'I'd hardly compare the two of you. You've given me something Charles couldn't.'

He went very still. 'You can't possibly know that yet.'

'I can sense it.' She sighed. 'I'm sorry now that we didn't get the short-term licence.'

'Three weeks isn't that long to wait.' He sounded odd. 'I'm not sure your mother's going to think this such a good idea.'

'I don't suppose she will.' Rachel wasn't yet wholly sure how *she* felt about it, just certain that she was right. 'Like everyone else, she'll have to accept it.'

'For Charles,' Craig said with irony. 'Duty done!' He turned her on her side, sliding an arm about her waist in an embrace that lacked warmth. 'Go to sleep.'

She did sleep eventually, but not until long after his breathing had deepened and the securing arm relaxed. Mentioning Charles at all had been a mistake, and one she wouldn't be making again. No more looking back from this point on.

The craft fair on Saturday was held in a school hall turned over for the purpose. With exhibitors from the mainland also taking part, the stalls were close-packed, even expanding into a couple of corridors. Regardless of the weather, which had broken the day before, or perhaps because of it, attendance was excellent. Almost from the moment the doors were opened at ten o'clock on the dot, the place was swarming with people.

Not all had come to buy, of course, as Laura pointed out. For some it was simply a way of spending a rainy Saturday morning under cover looking at interesting and beautiful things. Refreshments were on sale from the kitchens, with one of the nearby classrooms turned into a temporary diner. Very well-organised, Craig had commented earlier on, viewing the set-up. A credit to the event's committee.

He appeared to be enjoying himself, Rachel thought, watching him sell a large and garrulous Birmingham woman one of her mother's exquisite needle-point cushion-covers. Where the latter had found time and energy to write in addition to everything else she did was difficult to imagine. Rachel doubted if she could fit as much into life.

Congratulating her mother on the acceptance of her work, Rachel had been unable to refrain from questioning the lack of interest credited to herself. Just the way it had seemed, her mother had answered. Oversensitivity on her own part, perhaps. It just went to show how little one really knew of what went on in the minds of those even nearest and dearest.

'I still can't pretend to understand your wanting to marry a man as old as Charles,' she added candidly. 'And I certainly can't condone what he did in extracting that promise from you. You're lucky that Craig turned out to be the kind of man he is.'

The kind of man she still wasn't sure of, Rachel had reflected wryly. It was only at night, lying in his arms in the four-poster bed, that she could forget the limitations of their relationship. Having typed out the twelve-page synopsis he had already delivered, she could well believe that the novel which would grow from it would prove a winner. The question was whether having done it once he would be interested in doing another—or would he feel the urge to return to foreign fields? To lose him, even for a few weeks or months, would be devastating.

Lindsay and Keith showed up mid-afternoon. They had their pretty and lively little daughter with them. Rachel was enchanted by her—the more so because she had this inner certainty that the seed Craig had planted had already taken root. Unlike many men unaccustomed to children, Craig himself showed no self-consciousness in greeting her, gaining Lindsay's obvious approval.

'I see you got the Jag back,' commented Keith with a deceptively guileless look in his eyes. 'You do realise your tax disc is due for renewal the end of the month?'

Craig grinned, recognising the dig for what it was, and answering in like vein, 'Well spotted, Officer! A credit to the Force!' His glance went to Laura, at present standing idly by, waiting for the next customer. 'Would you be OK for a few minutes if we all went off for tea and a bun?'

'Of course,' she assured him. 'You've both been a tower of strength!'

'Two into one doesn't go,' he told her, tongue-in-cheek.

'Depends on the context,' she answered. 'Enjoy your tea, all of you.'

With the crowds beginning to dwindle, they managed to secure an empty table for the four of them. Gemma sat on her mother's lap, eyes lighting up on sight of the ice-cream cornet Craig brought back with the tray of tea and biscuits.

'No sticky buns left, I'm afraid,' he announced regretfully. 'It's been years since I last sampled one!'

'I'll make you some myself,' Rachel promised lightly. 'Though you'll have to wait for Mrs Johnston's day off. She hates me messing up her kitchen.'

'It must be nice to just order up what you fancy for meals, though,' said Lindsay a little wistfully. 'Standing over a hot stove three times a day isn't exactly my idea of heaven.'

'That's a hint for a new microwave,' observed Keith with mock resignation. 'I'm practised at picking up the vibes.'

His wife laughed. 'Practised at dodging the issue, you mean!'

Listening to the banter, watching the two faces, glancing at Gemma still happily spreading the ice-cream around her face, Rachel knew a very real envy. This was the kind of family life she wanted for herself, but was unlikely ever to have. It wasn't the venue that mattered so much as the depth of feeling involved. For Craig there was no depth, only desire.

It was Craig himself, however, who issued the invitation to come out to Apperknowle the following day, on learning that Keith was off-duty the whole weekend.

'According to the forecast, it's going to fine up again by morning,' he said. 'We could take a picnic down on the beach.'

'Gemma would like that.' Lindsay sounded surprised, but not averse.

'That's settled, then,' Rachel confirmed. 'Tomorrow it is.'

She and Craig eventually left for home at six-thirty, after helping her mother pack up what was left of her wares. The latter was having dinner with the friend who was going to be looking after Merlin's Cave while she was in London. Rachel had a feeling that the shop might have to take a back seat for a while, but no doubt her mother would work it out. She was, it seemed, capable of anything.

'It was nice of you to ask Lin and Keith over,' she said in the car.

'They're a nice couple,' Craig replied easily. 'More mature than most their age.'

Rachel gave him a sharp glance. 'Such as me?'

He laughed. 'Since when were you a couple? No ulterior meaning intended anyway. You're mature enough when you need to be.'

Rachel wasn't so sure. There had been times this past week or two when she had been less than adult in her reactions.

'If what you think turns out to be true,' he continued, 'I'll need to do some research into fatherhood. Keith seems to have it pretty well taped.'

'You intend being around quite a bit, then?' she asked carefully, and felt his eyes swing her way.

'Does the thought disconcert you?'

'You said that first day that being stuck on an island the size of this one for any length of time would bore you out of your mind,' she reminded him. 'The book probably won't take you longer than a few months.'

'Hopefully.' His tone was non-committal. 'We'll just have to see, won't we?'

No! she thought in sudden and emphatic rejection. She couldn't take that kind of uncertainty any longer.

'I'd rather have some idea of where we stand with regard to the future,' she said before she could lose courage. 'If you intend going back into journalism after this book is out of your system, then I want to know.'

It was a moment or two before he replied. When he did, it was on a note of constraint. 'What exactly would it mean to you if I did go away again?'

Rachel swallowed on the dryness in her throat. A straight question called for a straight answer, but she wasn't sure she was equal to it. To tell him she didn't want him to leave her was tantamount to acknowledging that her feelings went a whole lot deeper than his.

And yet was pride so important to her when it came right down to it? Wasn't the fact that she was probably going to have his child reason enough to want him with her? The love might be one-sided as yet, but it didn't have to stay that way. What was needed was time.

'Everything,' she admitted. 'I don't think I could bear it. Especially knowing what happened to you last time.'

They were through Godshill and heading in the direction of Chale Green. Craig brought the car to a stop at the roadside, and switched off the engine before turning to search her face with an intensity that brought sudden warmth flooding into her heart.

'Does that mean what I think it means—what I hope it means?' he asked.

Rachel managed a smile. 'If you're asking me do I love you, the answer is yes.'

'Thank God for that!' He was smiling himself now, arms coming out to draw her close. 'I was beginning to think I might have overplayed my hand.'

Still not wholly sure of what her senses were telling her, Rachel said softly, 'I don't understand.'

'I was afraid your feelings for me were limited to the physical.'

'That does have some bearing.' She studied the lean features with slowly increasing certainty and happiness. 'Didn't you intend it to have?'

'Of course. I set out to waken you up to what you'd obviously been missing with Charles.' He put his fingers to her lips as she made to speak, shaking his head. 'All right, so you really loved him. I'm prepared to accept that, as far as it goes. It still doesn't alter the fact that you'd never experienced full arousal.'

'Until you came along and showed me what it was all about,' she supplied. 'I suppose you're right, but it wasn't Charles's fault.'

'We won't argue about that.' His hand moved to caress her cheek with a touch so gentle that it made her ache. The grey eyes were warm and luminous. 'I arrived on the island expecting someone completely different. One look at you, and I was sunk.'

Rachel said huskily, 'You didn't make it obvious.'

'I wouldn't let myself believe it initially. All along I'd been convinced you were out for what you could get from a man you knew was dying. Having met you, and realised that it was unlikely, other factors took over. The very thought of you and him——' He broke off, shrugging wryly. 'It didn't make things any better when I saw the will. Especially the way you accepted it all. I made a vow there and then to jolt you out of it. To make you see the whole thing as something more than just a duty to be performed. Insisting on the marriage taking place right away was probably a mistake, but I couldn't just sit back and wait for six months. There was the chance that you might change your mind.'

'In which case you'd have lost everything.'

The momentary doubt was swiftly dispelled by the look in his eyes. 'Do you really think the money is so important to me?' he said roughly. 'I've got by fine up to now, and I'd go on doing it whatever. I wanted to tie things up because I was afraid of losing *you*, not the damned inheritance!'

It was Rachel's turn to put fingers to lips, this time in apology. 'I'm sorry, Craig. It's just...'

'It's just the way Charles set things up,' he finished for her as her voice trailed away. 'I've no means of proving what I say apart from withdrawing from the arrangement altogether. All you have is my word on how I feel about you.' He paused, gaze piercing her soul as he cupped her face between both his hands. 'And this——'

If there had been any faint doubt remaining, the kiss banished it forever. Rachel had never known such loving tenderness, such depth of emotion. She answered in kind, winding her arms about his neck in a burst of pure flooding ecstasy. There had never been, nor ever would be again, another man like Craig. Not for her!

'I believe you,' she whispered against his lips. 'I really do, Craig!'

'You'd better.' His voice was gruff. 'And while we're about it, I should tell you I've given up journalism. One of the things I decided while I was out there in the desert was that if I ever regained my freedom I'd call it a day and concentrate on novel-writing instead. I've used up most of my luck over the last ten years or so. I don't intend tempting providence too far. Anyway,' he added on a softer note, 'I've got something to stay home for now.'

Rachel's whole face was lit like a Christmas-tree. 'I'm so glad! I dreaded the thought of you going back to that life. This book will be a success. I know it will!'

Craig smiled. 'If not this one, then maybe another. The thing is to keep on trying. I'll hardly be starving in a garret while I'm doing it.'

'No, you'll be living at Apperknowle with your wife and children,' she said happily.

'Plural?' he queried with humorous inflexion. 'Isn't that looking rather a long way ahead?'

'Why not?' she asked. 'We're going to be together a long, long time.'

'Amen to that,' he said, and kissed her again, this time with a passion that threatened to take over. His breathing was unsteady when he at last raised his head, his eyes fired by desire. 'So let's get home and start laying the foundations.'

It was barely gone seven, Rachel thought fleetingly as he fired the ignition, but she didn't care either. There was no time limit on love.

HARLEQUIN®

PRESENTS *plus*

Meet Lewis Marsh, the man who walked out of Lacey's life twenty years ago. Now he's back, but is time really a cure for love?

And then there's widower Jim Proctor, whose young daughter, Maude, needs a mother. Lucy needs a job, but does she really need a husband?

These are just some of the passionate men and women you'll discover each month in Harlequin Presents Plus—two longer and dramatic new romances by some of the best-loved authors writing for Harlequin Presents. Share their exciting stories—their heartaches and triumphs—as each falls in love.

Don't miss
A CURE FOR LOVE by Penny Jordan,
Harlequin Presents Plus #1575
and
THE WIDOW'S MITE by Emma Goldrick,
Harlequin Presents Plus #1576

Harlequin Presents Plus
The best has just gotten better!

Available in August wherever Harlequin books are sold.
PPLUS3

Relive the romance...
Harlequin and Silhouette
are proud to present

by Request

A program of collections of three complete novels by the most
requested authors with the most requested themes. Be sure to
look for one volume each month with three complete novels by
top name authors.

In June: **NINE MONTHS** Penny Jordan
Stella Cameron
Janice Kaiser

**Three women pregnant and alone. But a lot can
happen in nine months!**

In July: **DADDY'S HOME** Kristin James
Naomi Horton
Mary Lynn Baxter

**Daddy's Home... and his presence is long
overdue!**

In August: **FORGOTTEN PAST** Barbara Kaye
Pamela Browning
Nancy Martin

**Do you dare to create a future if you've forgotten
the past?**

Available at your favorite retail outlet.

REQ-G